Eric Davidson has been a documentary film producer and drama director for many years, and holds a BAFTA award for documentary and a nomination for drama. He is a graduate in history, film and literary translation and has translated from French, German and Danish. He was awarded a grant from the Society of Authors to write *V for Schweik*.

GW00729029

V
FOR SCHWEIK

Eric Davidson

WARNER BOOKS

A *Warner* Book

First published in Great Britain in 1995
by Little, Brown and Company
This edition published by Warner Books in 1996

A CIP catalogue record for this book
is available from the British Library.

ISBN 0 7515 1621 X

Typeset by Palimpsest Book Production Limited, Polmont, Stirlingshire
Printed in Great Britain by Clays Ltd, St Ives plc

Warner Books
A Division of
Little, Brown and Company (UK)
Brettenham House
Lancaster Place
London WC2E 7EN

For Ted

If you want to get a big job out, get a little man in.

English Maxim

Contents

Foreword

In 1939 the men who went to war were, for the last time, the sons of Schweik, the heirs of Haslek's immortal Good Soldier: the common men, the small men, the botchers and the bunglers.

Most of them had no experience of war. All able-bodied men between eighteen and fifty, they came from the civvy street of the depressed Thirties and were bound together by Kitchener values and a Kipling sergeant. Bemused and baffled at once by the demands of war and the laws of loyalty and obedience, they accepted the hierarchy of social and military organisation and dutifully went over the top when told.

Their younger brothers who entered the war for the final phase from D-Day 1944 were another breed. By then all the older men had already been called up; and the only new recruits were those reaching the age of eighteen. These young men had been nurtured on war and the propaganda of war. It saturated all their information, in home, classroom, wireless, film, newspapers, comics and the whole gamut of everyday exchange. From 1939 *all* talk was of war.

At the same time these men had acquired their own knowledge of war through personal experience: in the blitzed streets of London and Liverpool, Coventry and Glasgow, Plymouth and Newcastle; and, evacuated from their families to makeshift homes on Devon farms and Welsh villages, alien schools and outlandish playgrounds, they had learned to survive the pain of separation – from fathers at the Front and mothers in munitions factories. They had become streetwise about war.

In one sense the stories in *V for Schweik* are *war* war stories, but in their origins they are Home Front stories, about growing up during a war and preparing *for* a war. The actions that occasion each of them evoke formative experiences of young men during their war years at home which shaped character and conditioned response at the Front.

In 1939 conscripted men came from all ages and were thrown in at the deep end with little idea of what was happening to them. By 1944 conscripted men were all young, boys nurtured for four years on the promotion of heroic deeds, imperial righteousness, the justness of the cause, and anti-Nazism. They reached puberty and maturity during wartime, so that when their turn came to serve they were wise about war and had had time to reflect on why they were going to it.

But they were still the heirs of Schweik.

ACROSS AND DOWN

The Channel, 6th June 1944

One

Somerset Mercy went to Normandy doing *The Times* crossword and searching for the clues that would give *him* a clue to his day.

'Come on, then, Somerset, let's have one! Anything to take our mind off this bleeding lot!'

The Infantry Landing Craft pitched in the angry Channel and a hundred soldiers retched. The wind moaned and the rain lashed across the decks.

'Right, then!' Somerset shouted against the opposition. 'Stand by!' He fought to balance himself against a bollard, one hand supporting him, the other clutching the folded *Times*. 'Two Down!' The boat shuddered to right herself and he shouted: '"Anything but a steady movement"! Seven letters!'

'Whoaaa, Somerset! Dead on!'

It was going to be one of these crossings.

The Russians were beleaguered in their own land; the U-boats were masters of the Atlantic supply routes. The Germans occupied the whole of Europe from Paris to Moscow and the enormous coastline of the continent was fortified throughout its entire length. The Allies had invaded in Sicily and Italy forcing the Germans to divert men from other fronts. But the real invasion, the proper Second Front, had still to take place. The question was how, where, and when?

On the mainland of Europe hundreds of thousands of German and coerced workers were frenziedly converting millions of tons of concrete and steel into one continuous fortress line along the entire coast. Did you invade by air or by sea? How did you conceive a plan and devise the technical needs to land two million men? How did you work out the logistics of what they would do once they got across? *And* how did you feed, clothe and arm them while they were there?

The solution was simple. The clue was the problem.

'Abomination!'

'Seven letters!' Somerset howled through the rain.

'Affliction!'

'*Seven*!' he screamed against the wind.

'Angels deliver us!'

'*One* word!' he roared above the engines.

'Agitate!'

'What's that got to do with a steady movement?' he asked quietly, puzzled.

'It fits, don't it!'

But at least the British were on their way.

As a young cub reporter Somerset Mercy designed crosswords for his local paper, the *Chard Print*, and did *The Times* crossword every morning in the hope that one day he would graduate to Fleet Street.

There was little of interest in the *Print* at the best of times – i.e. without a distracting war – apart from garden sheds and weddings, flower shows and cucumber competitions, and ads for second-hand lawnmowers. And as these had been severely restricted by the War Effort and the shortage of newsprint, Somerset had had to make his mark in journalism in an extremely confined space.

After eighteen months of pestering Mr Hamilton-Hanbury, the owner-editor, he was given a few column inches inside the back page alongside the obituaries. He took off. Within weeks his efforts were keeping up interest, circulation and peckers. But they were more than simple puzzles. They had a sort of religious purpose to them. Into each crossword 'Quicksilver' slipped clues to egg people on.

'Someone will find that *one* clue each day, see, and that will give him the design, and the paper the purpose.'

'Go on, then, give up. What's the solution?'

Somerset steadied himself against the Channel swell and studied the clue again. Through the damp spray he focused hard on:

2. *Anything but a steady movement.* (7)

Sure enough. It was doing it again.

'The solution doesn't matter,' he shouted absently.

'Screw that, man!' came the howl above the wind as the Channel stepped up its opposition. 'You telling us you just stare at these squares and it don't matter about filling them up?'

'It's not the important part. It's what your mind does when searching that counts.'

Personal solutions. What he had been preaching his readers for years.

For his own part Somerset had been studying the little black and white boxes in *The Times* for four years, willing the squares into a pattern, the clues into an attitude and the solutions into a message that would point towards him, and reveal that they had been composed according to *his* imprint, *his* design. Now, like a spinning roulette wheel, the blurred squares were coming to rest, the arrow opposite his number:

11. It's a bore when they come into action. (8)

Hadn't he always said that *Times* crosswords were only about personal solutions? Only the dull needed general ones to compare themselves to? Wasn't that precisely what he had been incorporating into 'Quicksilver' in the *Chard Print*?

'You mean it don't matter *what* you write in?'

'Of course it does! You try to find the correct solution but it only fits in a general sort of way. The object is the exercise. What matters is the journey, not the arrival.'

The boat shuddered and the men braced themselves. 'Oh yeah! Never mind what's ahead, just enjoy the trip!'

'Course!'

'Well, now, that *is* appropriate!'

'That's what I've been trying to bloody tell you!'

And the wave connected.

Somerset wasn't alone in his crossword agony.

In June 1941 Hitler had invaded Russia. In December the United States entered the war. The Allies in the West and the Russians in the East had a common enemy that lay in the middle. One day they would have to meet – somewhere, somehow. The object, the solution, was *pre*-determined. How to arrive at it, how to gather together the many elements and permutate them into a resolution that was rational and realisable, and then contort it into a code that would resist cracking until the final morning when it was printed, was the problem. As both Somerset and Eisenhower knew, the solution is one thing, the creation lies in the formulation of the clue.

The Allied High Command had been compiling their crossword for years, but it wasn't until Tuesday 6th June 1944 that they published their solution:

Invasion of Normandy.

The landing craft struggled to find even keel.

'Don't take it literally,' shouted Somerset. 'Work at it and you'll find other things coming up.'

The boat pitched and a hundred men retched.

'See what you mean!'

Another wave hit them amidships and knocked the boat askew. One second they were pitching forward, the next they were taking an almighty thump to their ribs.

From Friday 15th September 1939 when he was fourteen and a week until Tuesday 6th June 1944 when he was eighteen and eight months, Somerset had lived by *The Times* crossword: followed it like a catechism or zodiac chart, a set of rules or a horoscope. *The Times* crossword told him all he needed to know, and contained all he needed to find.

'If you lot would pay attention you'd get what you need from it as well.'

'Give us another clue, then. But make it an easier one this time.'

Somerset scanned the softening lump in his hand as the rain supplemented the spray.

'Fancy an anagram?' he shouted.

'Why not. Haven't tasted one for ages.'

'One word. Nine letters.'

'Go on, then!'

Another squall threatened his *Times*.

'Rains cats!' he roared.

Somerset Mercy first met *The Times* crossword on his way down to Somerset by train from Waterloo the day he was evacuated from Ealing in September 1939. He was distracted by the master in charge of the carriage who was far more absorbed in his newspaper than his duties, swaying with the rock of the train, struggling to retain a perpendicular stance, avoiding the clamour and demands of the hundred children he was supposed to be taking care of, and scribbling earnestly on his folded newspaper.

Somerset, who was plain George then, sat fascinated, huddled up in raincoat and thick jersey with his gas-mask case slung around his neck and resting on his knees. And he wondered what a grown-up could be so engrossed in when all around the world was at war and dads were being torn from their families and deported, and children from their mums and deported.

Behind them lay mothers and aunts and sisters wailing and waving on the platform at Waterloo, and beyond *them* lay houses and homes and cats and dogs and rabbits and guinea pigs from which they were being so unnaturally wrenched because everyone said the Germans were on their way; and even at that moment George imagined them jackbooting their way into his bedroom and mucking about with his printing set.

Yet, despite all that calamity, this strange man in his dark brown suit and trench coat and trilby and moustache and matching horn-rimmed glasses was determined that, Germans or no Germans, he would finish what he was doing.

George watched him twitching and turning and sucking his pencil and scribbling notes down the side of the paper and beaming when he wrote in something positive. He could see it was a crossword puzzle but a schoolmaster would have done the crossword puzzles he was used to in five minutes, if he bothered at all.

When he did finish, he turned to vent his wrath on his charges for misbehaving while he was concentrating. But George, 'Quicksilver' to be, intervened, daring to ask him what was in his paper that was so absorbing. Mr Leslie Dilberry was so taken aback his wrath evaporated in a twinkling, and he sat down, astonished at this request, and spread before the infatuated George the wonders, mysteries and challenges of *The Times* crossword.

And there it stood, 1 Across, in *The Times* crossword, No. 2,986, the clue that was to set him on a new path into a new world leaving behind his native green for the jackbooted Nazis to parade on and his Caxton's Mark 11 printing set for them to violate:

1. The flower of periodical journalism. (5, 6)

Mr Dilberry explained the solution:

Hardy Annual

But George wasn't interested in the solution, only in the message. It stood out from the page like a beacon summoning him on, challenging him. The only crossword clues he had ever seen demanded simple meanings for words. This was another kind of puzzle, like a jigsaw with words, only much more.

As Mr Dilberry was explaining how the clues were formulated, George's eye was roaming:

20. Very much a bird of passage. (5, 3)

That was him all right. Never mind the solution.

11. It is to be borne by him who has deserved it. (4)
11 Palm

Well, well!

George was already elsewhere. Something personal was shining through: predictions and omens that no crossword compiler could ever have thought of before. And long before he reached his destination, Nazi jackboots and Ealing Green were already far behind, and the future 'Quicksilver' of the *Chard Print* was on his way to Somerset, *The Times* crossword, a niche in the local rag, and a place in a landing craft bound for the Normandy beaches.

'What's the solution, then, Somerset?'

The progress across the Channel was slow. The weather set for lousy.

'Which one?' asked Somerset absently, more absorbed now in the other clues that were emerging:

9. *'Go lovely rose.'(—) (6)*

The Great Compiler never failed, you know.

'The "rains cats" or the "steady movement"?' he asked.

'Both.'

14. *The forty ninth was dramatised. (8)*

'It's up to you.'

'Aw, c'mon! The *correct* one!'

'There *is* no *correct* one. Only a general, standard one.'

'Who cares what you bloody call it! Just put us out of our agony, will you? Isn't seasickness enough?'

28. *It would be just after me.*

'I can't. It's not given until tomorrow.'

'Tomorrow! There might not *be* a bloody tomorrow!'

Somerset stood his ground, or rather held tight as the rolling went on and the wind freshened and the sky darkened and he read 20 Across:

Cut down colour. (3)

Indeed.

'Don't they print it on the back?'

'*The Times* crossword *is* on the back.'

'What bleedin' good is that!'

'Printing solutions on the same day admits there *are* universal solutions. Misses the whole point. *Times* crosswords are about each man finding his own.'

'But you say they print it the following day in any case!'

'That's another matter. It no longer *means* anything.'

'What do they print it for then?'

'For those who only see it as a pastime, an escape.'

They heaved over and the groans vied with the moaning of the wind. Somerset's eye fell on:

> 24. *Torturers did not add insult to injury by charging this up to their victims.* (8)

Of course. And he was unrepentant.

'Each puzzle is always a new beginning', he raved on, 'a singular arrangement of design and words that relates only to today.'

His eye fell on a watery

> 13. *Blessed in poetry.* (7)

and felt it fitted the sentiment.

The journey down from Waterloo changed George's life. It changed his name to Somerset for a start. The name intrigued him, the sound and the combination of images – 'summer' and 'set': 'summer' as in all things bright and beautiful, and 'set' as in fixed and permanent. There was a romance in the name: it belonged to Wild West movies and wide-open spaces. As the train steamed on through the countryside, everything seemed to be green and wide and open and far, all words that had figured little in George's vocabulary or experience in Ealing, although they did have a common and a green. But back there it was *a* green; here it was green.

As the fields rolled past and the thoughts came tumbling in, the idea was planted that maybe after all he wouldn't want to go to war if and when his time ever came; maybe he would just hide away in this strange new peace he had never known.

Mr Dilberry was pointing to:

> 16. *A photograph of Miss Rogers?*
> *She's accustomed to something more elaborate.* (10)

and telling him the answer:

gingersnap

Ah!

With this new-found vision that was calming his nerves, dampening his fears of the unknown, and taking away the pain of parting, went the discovery of this other land – *The Times* crossword.

Mr Dilberry was explaining it as 'mental gymnastics', which sounded like something you did in a drill hall, but all George knew was that you could do it on your own, even standing up in a crowded train. If you could go this deep into yourself and not need anyone to guide and command you then you could be warm and absorbed on your own whatever lay ahead. He knew he would cope.

This war might have its compensations yet.

The boat lurched and Somerset surveyed his charges. Well, they were hardly *his* and hardly *charges* but he felt a twinge of responsibility, as if somehow he had been entrusted with the duty of promoting confidence and morale, a cross between padre and palmist.

Somerset, the Allied High Command, and the men around him all had something in common with *The Times* crossword compiler. As he peered through the spray and saw only white horses rearing before him, he knew the clue was

1. Second Front

but they had taken years to decide where it should appear on the grid, whether it should be across or down, and how many letters. Like they knew now the solution was '*France*' but where, and across or down, and quote, anagram or plain teaser? '*France*' was only a general solution.

'What about the easy one you done for us, Somerset?' a voice called above the increased roar as the propellers lifted clear of the water.

Somerset came out of his reverie and took out the smeared roneo copy of another puzzle.

On that journey down from Ealing with Mr Dilberry, George had found his eyes glazing as Mr Dilberry talked on. The black and white squares began to make weird patterns as if Mr Dilberry's hand underneath was turning and spinning them like a kaleidoscope. He saw shapes forming, ornamental patterns and curves and crosses sending out messages in ancient script in history books and carved on stones in museums.

They began to tell George things: that *Times* crosswords are devices to tell you more than appears at first glance, suggestions and intimations, clues to the reader's day and destiny. And symbols: emerging from the patterns, together with the words, to give clues to what you were doing with your life that day, forcing you to reflect and not treat each day as some tedium to be got through but as a period of time to be experienced.

George went into journalism to impart this knowledge. He began to devise his own mini-*Times* crossword to give readers a new beginning and himself an interest, and to take his mind off the pain of being wrenched from his mother and father and sisters and friends.

When he boarded the landing craft at Portsmouth on 6th June 1944 armed with his Enfield and his sheaves of crossword papers, Somerset had not the slightest doubt that he was fulfilling a role. Today would be his greatest challenge.

Mr Dilberry would have been proud, perhaps a little envious too, that he had only ever seen the upside, however intricate and subtle, of the blessed *Times* crossword.

And the first clue that caught his eye that morning was
5 Across:

E'en from the — the voice of nature cries (Gray). (4)

'Oh, hoh,' he sighed, and wrote in

TOMB.

He had done his own for D-Day, one for the others,
because he knew they'd never stick through *The Times*.
In fact he had only used a few *Times* teasers as warm-
ers up.

He had made it up of all the reasons they were
there in this place at all: like hope, glory, bully beef,
king, country, spam, freedom, free food, fear, travel and
general interest. The way the weather looked they should
get it done well before sight of any beach.

But he hadn't reckoned on the seasickness.

'Enough to put you right off your concentration.'

'All right,' he called, consulting the damp paper. 'Let's
go! Seven Across, seven letters beginning with D and,
wait for it, the clue is: "D-Day"!'

His voice rose above the complaint of the engines and
the irritated Channel.

'Disastrous!'

'Seven letters!'

'Desperate!'

'*Seven*!'

'Depressing!'

'Dreadful!'

'Drop Dead!'

The waves chopped and changed and defied all
attempts to establish any hope of a rhythm to the
crossing . . . or even the crossword.

'Destruction!'

'*Seven* letters!'

'Damnation!'

'Damn your eyes!'

Raucous replies gathered beneath the huddle of bobbing helmets.

'Up yours!'

And threatened to erupt and disturb the peace of the summer crossing.

'Dire!'

'*Seven* letters!' Somerset wouldn't yield. His clear voice struggled to keep above the uneven roar of the landing craft's engines.

'Drab!'

'*One* word! *And it's seven* letters!'

'And so is my . . . !'

The voice remained defiant and determined. Somerset was not to be denied his hour.

From that first crossword No. 2,986 on the train from Waterloo to No. 4,450, when he embarked for Normandy, Somerset had lived with one thousand, four hundred and sixty-four of them.

He had savoured every one. He hadn't solved them but he had studied them and taken from them far more than the mundane solutions of the day. He soon stopped viewing the 'correct solution' the following morning. He had treated each one of the fourteen hundred and sixty-four as unique: particular and personal.

Even as he closed his eyes now and the spray of the Channel mingled with the rain and the heaving of the landing craft and the cries of the sick and the roars of overhead aircraft that seemed to darken the skies more than the clouds, Somerset felt at peace, surprised now he wasn't surprised, that he had established such a deep relationship with these anonymous compilers over the years of evacuation. They had become kindred minds in his loneliness. Fought many a tussle with them. Never won, but so what? He'd long since acknowledged he didn't want to *win*. Not in *that* sense. Not in the sense of beating someone, defeating him. Like running and jumping and football. The compiler merely points the way. The rest is up to you.

He opened his eyes, shook his head, and scrutinised the wet page, admiringly mesmerised by the ceaseless virtuosity of compilers.

> 9. *'Go lovely rose.'* (—) *(6)*

Yes, yes.

That very first journey from Waterloo spoke to him with clues like:

> 25. *Put me in the lane but it isn't coming back. (6)*

and

> 19. *This qualifies one for palm. (5)*

and inspired by the very first one he ever set eyes on:

> 1. *The flower of periodical journalism. (5, 6)*

he went to the offices of the *Chard Print*, while still at school, with three essays and a sample crossword, and offered his services to Mr Hamilton-Hanbury. Aitch-Aitch took him on: 'I cannot pay you, you understand', he encouraged George, 'and newsprint is damned scarce these days, but you are welcome to hang about.' Long before he left school, George, or Somerset as he now thought of himself, was already well versed in journalism and indulging his passion for words with the ease of a country vicar who wrote Latin verse as a hobby having no pressure on him but the demands of God on Sundays. It took his mind off the war, the pain of separation, and the knowledge that one day he would be called up too.

'Well, war can have its compensations,' observed Aitch-Aitch, believing he had personally rescued another lost refugee.

By the time he came to see Normandy in his sights in the middle of the Channel just before 2 Down, Somerset had had three solid years of apprenticeship on the *Chard Print* and established his own particular niche and byline: the famous 'Quicksilver' crossword that 'gives you clues in more ways than one'.

11. *It is to be borne by him who has deserved it.* (4)

palm

Of course.

'What is it then, Somerset? Destiny? Desperate? Disastrous?'

The voices came at him through a veil of rain and wind, and the engines roared and the floor shuddered like a train braking. It *was* like being back on a train again. Things were green too. But he didn't notice the cold.

'Dreadful Day! Depressing Day!'

He heard the cries all right. But what did the answer matter? They were concentrating.

'Watch it, lads, looks as if Somerset's going to heave up!'

'Design Day,' he had written. Like every crossword is a design, so every day has its design and you have your design too. D-Day, Dog's Day, Design Day – it's all a design.

'Quicksilver' proved a success and sales of the *Chard Print* rocketed to 'far and away beyond our print allocation,' said Aitch-Aitch.

People were buying the paper who had usually been only too able to leave it alone. They became addicted to the unique brand of brain challenge and mystery, without knowing why.

'Still, mustn't grumble,' said Aitch-Aitch each week

as the paper sold out again. 'As I said, war has to have some compensations.' But Aitch-Aitch refused to admit that 'Quicksilver' was any more than a 'flash in the pen'. Nevertheless when Somerset suggested he might be leaving for a better job on the *Budleigh Bugle*, he very quickly offered to increase his expenses for all the research he had to do brushing up on general knowledge, literature and astrology, and keeping abreast of the ever-increasing body of national and world events. Somerset stayed on because he wanted to anyway, and for the peace to do his own *Times* crossword each day, to keep himself fit and in trim for the day when the call might come for him.

The crossword in his hand now was the roneoed one with his own compilation, made up of all the reasons they were here. They hadn't got very far. Maybe that was a clue, if not an answer. At least he knew why *he* was here. It was his turn.

It was like we had two wars – the one that started in 1939 and went on right up to Cassino; and the one that was starting now, here on this bouncing boat surrounded to the horizons by swarms of similar craft like shoals of black migrating whales, and would go on right up to Berlin.

The first seemed like the old war, the one he had been evacuated from in 1939, the one that had rescued him. As Aitch-Aitch said: the one that had compensations. He had had his. And not just fought and finished, but fought on old standards and principles, if you could ever have principles in war. Rules of combat, rules of engagement, of course, but principles? Sounding meaningless out here in the wind and rain and swell with god knows what ahead.

Can you kill according to rules? According to principles? Course not. A vulgar deception, he thought, and made a note of it for a future crossword. Through the spray he saw the clue:

Rules of war. (6, 9)

and the solution:

vulgar deception

War can only be an aspect of failure, he was thinking as a low-flying bomber thundered him out of his daydream.

He glanced down at his wet *Times* and noted:

16. It is only practised to deceive. (9)

Better still. Always on the ball, isn't he?

What would be the rules of this one? Any clues?

Must get it done before we land. Always a challenge to get it done before the day's work is started, or over. When you complete it, it makes sense. You can rest in peace, then.

Aloud he was saying: 'It doesn't matter anyway. Nothing to do with war. Just get it finished! Get an order into things! Or *the* order!'

'Come along, Somerset! Wakey wakies!'

Design Day. Weird, in a way. And yet not. Not *ever*, in fact. You don't get simple coincidences in the *Times*. I mean, miles of bloody beach ahead of us and look what he comes up with:

31. Sandy site for houses. (9)

I ask you!

'You all right, mate?' An iron hand gripped his shoulder as he kept staring at the wet paper and shaking his head.

'Anagram of "dynasties", I expect. But that's not the point!'

'Best get rid of it before we land. You'll feel a lot better.'

'But, I've got my . . .' and he held up the clumps of sodden paper.

'Keep 'em for later. The blokes have got their minds on other things.'

'But there aren't any *other* things,' he protested, brandishing his *Times*.

'Blimey, still wrestling with the old enemy, are we?'

'*Enemy*? He's not an *enemy*!'

'Well, for a friend he's certainly given you a tough time on the way over.'

The noise was intense suddenly. He hadn't noticed.

'*Pro*-tagonist. Never *an*!'

'Whatever. Blokes like us need solutions, I'm afraid.'

'That's a mockery!'

'More helpful, though.'

'That means a general solution for everybody!'

'Tidier too.'

'Takes away the mystery.'

'But it don't half make for a neat ending.'

'*The Times* crossword isn't *about* neat endings! Nothing in life has a neat ending!'

'Suit yourself, of course.'

9. 'Go lovely rose.' (—) (6)

'Just look at that!' Somerset said admiringly to no one in particular. He had no doubts now. The compiler was strengthening his resolve, scattering clues, adding his own initials, his personal mark, like mediaeval scribes signing illuminated manuscripts, masons marking cathedral stones, goldsmiths engraving hallmarks. Enemy indeed!

The noise was intense now. The bombers seemed dangerously low. Can't hear yourself think.

'Stand by, men!'

He heard that well enough. But still one to go. The waves pulled back from the beach and the boat heaved as a hundred men steadied themselves to take the strain of the blow and the bombers seemed to be landing on top of them.

Somerset read:

27. Shot in the chest. (8)

and said aloud: 'He's very neat, isn't he?'

STILL LIFE

Caen, July 1944

Two

Brush Morgan had seen more of the war than anyone else of his age long before he reached the outskirts of Caen and pulled out his sketch pad. In his mind's eye he had witnessed it in clear colourful detail, and in even more clear colourful detail he had depicted it on every scrap of paper he had been able to lay his paint-stained fingers on, ever since the Germans bombed Warsaw in August 1939 when he was thirteen and a half until he joined the attack on Caen on 20th July 1944 when he was eighteen and a half.

One sunny morning in late August 1939 Brush sat huddled and preoccupied over his *Hotspur* and cornflakes and heard the reverberating click-thump of his father's *Daily Express* thrusting through the letter-box and landing on the carpet. The noise shook him alert. He had heard that sound a thousand times without ever looking up. But this morning it registered and stopped him reading and eating. He got up and walked to the door. The paper had fallen open and staring up at him were the sinister silhouettes of German Stuka dive-bombers screaming their way vertically down towards Warsaw below; while similar dark shapes of heavy Heinkels hovered above the city and unloaded their blocks of black death on to the packed buildings out of the frame.

The grandfather clock in the hall click-clocked to a crescendo as Brush watched the bombs fall and pass on out of the picture on to the buildings below and then through on to the groups of women and children huddled beneath, groping for life in the basements and makeshift shelters, grasping for futile protection against the flying monsters and their cargoes of death and destruction.

'What's up?' said his mother, coming into the hall and noticing him standing there transfixed. 'Breakfast not to your taste, then?'

'The pictures,' Brush managed, still staring.

Brush had missed the landings at Normandy but, like the rest of his age group, he knew it was to be his war from then on. From Dunkirk to Cassino, through Tobruk, Alamein and Anzio, dads, big brothers and uncles had all done their bit. Now it was the turn of the next generation, the younger sons and brothers who had been quietly preparing for it in their classrooms and air-raid shelters, and behind their blackouts and makeshift window screens; and who had been less quietly prepared for it in their evacuation centres and drill halls, gas-mask rehearsals and fire-fighting practices, through bill boards and advertising campaigns, newsreels, wireless programmes, cinema, and the whole planned paraphernalia of war-time propaganda.

They had always known they would be going to war. They had heard nothing else in their lives *but* war. So if they had had more time to worry about it, they had also had more time to prepare for it. Unlike their dads, uncles and big brothers who had been called up in 1939 and whipped off to Dunkirk before they could finish packing and without any idea of what they were supposed to do or why they were supposed to be doing it, Brush's generation had been bred for war. From Normandy on it would be their war and their job, as the jargon described it, to 'finish it off'.

But of all his generation, Brush Morgan was more prepared than most.

'What pictures?' asked Brush's mother, pushing him aside and picking up the paper lying below the letter-box. 'Oooh, them bloody Germans again!' She looked at them cursorily but saw only the aircraft. 'I tell you, never trust a bloody Boche, as my old dad always used to say. And he should have known. They got him at Wipers. Come on,' she berated him, 'get on with your breakfast or you'll be late.'

Brush went back to the table but didn't finish eating. 'What's up with you, lad?' said his mother, worried at his vague look. 'Gone all pale, you have.'

Brush continued to stare at the paper open in her hand. She looked down and said, 'Well, they're only machines. Creepy enough, mind you, but still only machines.'

'No, the other ones,' Brush muttered.

His mother reached over and picked up the paper. '*What* other ones?' she asked.

'Down below.'

She squinted at the picture of bombers flying high over a city. And all she saw of the city was the spires of churches and the rooftops of high buildings running along the bottom of the frame like the squiggles of jagged rocks.

'Below what?' she asked, irritably.

'Below the bombers.'

'Can't see nothing more.'

'The women and children in the shelters.'

She looked at Brush then picked up the paper again and studied the page. But she could see only the black shapes of the aircraft and their bomb loads hurtling down. 'Can't see no women or children there!' she said.

Brush stared down into his sagging cornflakes and watched them slowly disappear beneath the surface of the milk like wedding confetti sinking in the gutter on a wet Saturday.

'Oh?' he said and, pushing back his chair and rising, walked off to school leaving behind his stained *Hotspur* and drowning cornflakes.

Brush's first real taste of action came at dead of night on Thursday 6th July, 1944, when he was shipped in with a fresh group of reinforcements to supplement Monty's Eighth in 'Operation Goodwood'. In thick darkness they struggled into position on Hill 62 just outside Caen and were ordered 'to keep . . . bleedin' heads down . . . get killed 'cos running . . . out of spares . . . can't afford . . . lose no more of you lot . . . till Monday, see!' the sentence badly fractured by the awful din of war all around them.

He found himself head down in a hole of sorts or a ditch with overhanging shrubs, and wedged in beside him, like kittens snuggling into their mother, was a mound of moaning, squirming, terrified infantrymen like himself. The only difference was that Brush was silent and calm, indifferent even, and the others were moaning and whining as if they had already been assaulted and were grade one casualties waiting to be shipped out.

Not that he was courageous. He had just seen it all before. And when dawn broke – or caved in – after five hours of black terror in the dank ditch, the sight that emerged before his eyes was exactly like he had seen in thousands of pictures since that first war-torn Warsaw five years before. Below him on the ridge: dust, debris and rubble down to the far horizon; and dust, debris and rubble from distant left to faraway right; highways, farm roads, farmbuildings, streets, houses and churches, razed, reduced, ruined; trees like broken matchsticks, buildings like erupted volcanoes; one leviathan lorryload of rubbish tipped over the wasted landscape of Caen, dust still smouldering from the pile and hovering all over it like a protective halo signalling it had only just landed. A war artist's dream.

That Monday morning Brush walked straight into his art class at school and set to work. From that moment of revelation he knew that war was about something else.

'What's this, then, Morgan?' asked Mr Feber, who had fought on the Somme.

Head down in intense concentration Brush was covering his paper with drawings of women and children in fear and torment amid the rubble of devastated rooms decorated with splintered sticks of furniture and shredded mattresses; and of pulverised houses decorated with the distorted limbs and mutilated torsos of fragmented women and children.

'Warsaw, sir,' said Brush, authoritatively, not pausing to look up.

'And where do you get these images from, may I ask?'

'Newspaper, sir.'

'Oh, indeed! And what newspaper would that be, pray?'

'The *Express*, sir. My dad always takes the *Express*, sir.'

'I get the *Express* too, Morgan, but I doubt I have seen the likes of this in *my* copy!'

'Oh, it's there, all right, sir.'

Mr Feber, always an admirer of Brush's talent and imagination, but now disconcerted and apprehensive, looked up to see the rest of the class clustered around and gasping at Brush's vivid display.

'Now look here, back to your seats and get on with your own work!' he barked, ushering them away from the quarantined zone around Morgan's desk. Confounded, he looked back down at Brush relentlessly covering the sheet with brains, broken bones, free floating arms, swirling legs and fingers flying wildly across a space that had once been a bedroom and kitchen. He hurried to his desk and returned with his copy of the *Express* and spread it before Brush, saying, 'Bombers over Warsaw, I grant you, Morgan. Stukas and Heinkels and bombs, yes. But no carnage or devastation like that! Not in *my Express*!'

'It's there, Mr Feber,' said Brush assuredly, without taking his eyes off his painting, and stabbing the newspaper picture with his left hand. 'Must be.' And pointing to the bombs, he added, 'That shows them going down. Mine here shows them arriving. Can't have one without the other, can you?' And for the first time, he paused to look up at the ageing art teacher and said, 'But *you* know that, Mr Feber. You been and seen them things, haven't you?'

Stung in his tracks, Mr Feber went silent and distant and stared down at the back of Brush's head hunched over the lurid painting. And as he did so he found his eyes defocusing so that they presented to him an image of raw flesh and discharged blood oozing out from all around Brush's head as if from his own brain.

'Besides,' said Brush, 'you're always telling us to use our imagination, aren't you, Mr Feber?'

With the coming of daylight, the scene emerged reluctantly, pushing aside its blanket as if embarrassed at what it had to reveal. But Brush studied it calmly, professionally holding a twig before his eyes like an artist with his pencil, and moving it around like a telescope to settle on various components of the view.

As he squinted his eyes to pin-point a clutch of burnt-out Bren-gun carriers squeezed together to form a pyramid of steel, a single shell screamed towards him and exploded on the hill. He kept his right hand reaching before him to the target and dropped his face down into the wet sod, pressing his helmet to his head with his left hand like a woman holding her hat in the breeze. After a few seconds came a pulverising crump and Brush took the shock of a huge weight thrust against him. He counted another twenty seconds, checked for the sensation of his left hand on his helmet and ticked it off, then checked for the sensation of his right hand still thrusting out to measure the devastation down below the hill, and ticked that off too. After another few seconds he opened his eyes and turned to his left. By his side three corpses formed a stylised pyramid like the wrecked Bren carriers.

He studied them calmly as if used to seeing such formations every morning, then he looked back along the line of his right arm at the distant Bren formation. For a few moments he moved his eyes between the two structures, then pulled his right arm back in and calmly reached into his pack to pull out a sketching block.

All the while the screams of other men in pain on that hill reeled around him. But Brush heard nothing. Nor did he hear anything of the other kind of screams from his corporal. Brush had been well trained. He had learned his discipline in a hard school.

'You always tell me to draw what's in my mind, Mr Feber,' said Brush, when the well-meaning but troubled master tried to get him to 'tone it down a bit', or even to try another subject 'just for a break. I mean, everyone has to have a spot of leave sometime, doesn't he?' he said.

'That's what I'm doing,' Brush replied, pointing to a disemboweled soldier being shovelled into a hole with a farm fork which he entitled *Early Harvest*.

By the time his turn came to join up in early 1944, Brush's home and box-room were covered in gargoyles:

'Goya Gargoyles' as his schoolmates called them after the art teacher's horror.

At first everyone had got very worried once that Warsaw picture had unleashed his deep feelings. Family, friends, teachers and doctors came to discuss and examine him, but Brush had answers for them all, and with such calm clarity and sweet reasonableness that they couldn't find a respectable reason to cart him away, which they obviously dearly wanted to do, if only because of the shame.

They tried to coax and cajole him. 'Why don't you rest a bit and take it easy? You can overdo schoolwork too, you know.'

They bribed him with extra butter and sugar rations. 'Go on, take it. It's not black market. And we know you love the stuff.'

They asked continually if he was feeling unwell again. 'Would you like an aspirin or a Beecham's, a Uneeda headache powder, maybe, or a Painban? They're new and supposed to be very good.'

But no, Brush needed none of that. 'I could do with some more paint, though.'

They tried to hide his drawings and shield them from the other children, but that wasn't easy because Brush never considered there was a conspiracy against him and therefore took no effort to hide what he was doing or deny what was in his mind.

'It's just what comes out, Mr Feber, sir,' he would say as he generously spread blood around his page. And brains. Brush was good at brains. There were lots of brains in Brush's pictures, usually idly scattered brains, slopped over tank sides or Jeep bonnets.

And limbs. 'Why so many limbs?' Mr Feber said, not having anything more to contribute. 'You seem to like limbs.' And sure enough, they were draped everywhere, decorating the pages like wisps of wheat or branches, or bushes torn asunder in the wind. But he brooked no innuendo.

'They're not *limbs*, Mr Feber. They're legs! Legs and arms and feet and fingers, see?'

'Yes, not much attempt to be subtle, is there, Morgan?'

'Oh, no, sir! Like you always tell us: be direct. No bones about it.'

Brush worked on coolly amid the chaos on Hill 62. All around him raged panic and pandemonium. The reinforcements had been taken completely off guard, as had the Commands that had called for them and placed them there.

There was no end to the evidence. It was a painter's paradise. Brush's charcoal raced across the pages. Everywhere he turned there was another instance of horror, another splodge of brains, another pattern of limbs. He worked on completely engrossed.

The battle for Caen was virtually over. The most important road junction in Normandy, and the bastion of Rommel's defence line in the east, had fallen to British tanks and infantry from the north and Canadian troops from the west. The Germans, or what was left of them, were on their way south, abandoning the rubble to the invaders. And the combined allied forces of British, American, Canadian and Polish troops were in pursuit, pressing on to force the retreating Germans into the Falaise gap, the bottleneck of that corridor of hell that would end the campaign in northern France begun exactly one month before with the D-Day landings.

There was no one to expect a counter attack on Hill 62 or anywhere else. Yet something had gone wrong. Something unexpected and uncalculated for had turned up.

'Something *always* goes bloody wrong!' moaned a hardened campaigner of four weeks. 'Something unexpected and uncalculated for *always* turns up! What the bleeding

hell do you expect in a war that *we're* fighting? Organisation? Plans that *work*, for Christ sake!'

Whatever, the stray shells from a German unit that
shouldn't, *couldn't* have been in that sector had done
their damage, and dumbfounded those left alive. Except
Brush. Brush never got dumbfounded. 'Why don't you
dumbfound like the rest of us, Morgan?' a corporal had
once asked during training.

'Dunno, corp,' he had shrugged. 'Nothing surprises
me, I suppose.'

'You always been like that?'

'Maybe.'

On Hill 62 the survivors were so dumbfounded
they couldn't believe Brush. Two bloodstained, mud-
spattered men were detailed by the still full-voiced
corporal to 'stack all bodies aside at the double' into
some temporary shelter to await the 'bleeding bastard
collection party', and came across Brush, cross-legged
in his ditch, carefully and intently engrossed in his
charcoal study. Open-mouthed, they watched as this
soiled apparition kept raising and dropping his pencil
like a wind-up toy to sight the formation before him
and then apply it to the gleaming pad on his knees.
They might never have moved out of their frozen posture
but the scream from the corporal to 'move your bleeding
bastard arses!' coaxed them from their traumatised inertia
to move forward to the three bodies.

But the second they broke, Brush's hand whipped up
and out to them, pencil point directed to their eyes like a
sharpened pistol and, charged with awesome authority,
his voice stabbed out, 'Don't dare! Fuck off!'

In absolute disbelief and fear, the pair froze, backed,
turned and ran. Brush dismissed their mad screams from
his mind as easily as he dismissed all the other noises of
war about him.

*   *   *

At school, Brush Morgan became an institution, and a problem. Or rather a problem, then an institution.

After that first day in the art class, he never looked back. He had found his war, or rather his part in it. He had always displayed some talent in drawing and painting and, if not Mr Feber's prize pupil, he was certainly one of his brighter sparks. But hitherto he had been what Mr Feber described as a messy sort of student.

'It's not only your drawing, Morgan, it's the organisation of your work.'

'Yes, sir.'

'You start off well enough and then seem to go off the rails, smearing your charcoal and colours all over the place.'

'Yes, sir.'

'I mean, I can see you may be trying for impressionistic effects but impressionism demands its own discipline, you know. It's not a mere matter of smudging materials over the canvas.'

'No, sir.'

'Soft focus is a cultivated, artistic effect, not an uncontrolled by-product. Try keeping your elbows off the painting for a start.'

But whatever Brush tackled he quickly gave up. His concentration span was severely restricted. Five minutes into a kettle and he switched into dawdle mood. Three minutes into an orange and he was deep in smudge.

'I sometimes get the feeling you are not entirely in sympathy with your subject, Morgan.'

'No, sir.'

'I mean, still life is not one of your fortes, is it?'

'Pardon, sir?'

'Never mind. Maybe we shall have to find something a trifle more appealing.'

The day war broke out, Brush found his trifle. The day

he focused in on the *Daily Express* Stukas, he focused in on himself. Brush had found his subject and his purpose.

The corporal arrived next and was so stunned by the unearthly spectacle of Brush and the three corpses that his blasphemy deserted him and he sank to the ground and stared at the group, neither appalled nor disbelieving, troubled nor angry.

Brush worked coolly and calmly. The other members of his platoon had either died of bullets or shrapnel or fright. But he worked on amid the chaos. He had lived through it for five years. He was the only one there who was even remotely prepared for what he encountered.

The corporal sat fazed, rock still and stone silent. Brush was oblivious of his audience. He studied the corpses and then moved his head left and right as if watching a game of tennis in slow motion. The corporal mechanically followed.

The noises of war reached them thickly from far beyond the hill, as if from a conflict taking place in another country. And they reached them from the other side of the shrub and bushes where the remnants of the reinforcements tried to piece themselves together in the absence of the only leader left, their corporal; but it was less a sound of war than a low whimpering of farm dogs, cowed, abandoned, waiting.

Only once did the corporal make a move, to adjust his position on the wet grass. And Brush, suspecting out of the corner of his eye that he might be about to disturb his model, leapt from his macabre study and thrust out his dagger pencil like a sabre staying the move in mid action. But the corporal froze and the wrath of art was assuaged.

Mr Feber became an unwilling accomplice.

From the moment of Brush's revelation, he had become

a disruptive influence. He may have found his war, or his part in it; he may have found what Mr Feber himself would have called his focus, but he was against the spirit of war. And in the Britain of the 1940s that was a traitorous thing to be. The war may have been advertised as evil, but everything the nation did in it was noble. God was on our side. Brush obviously wasn't. He was making war something obscene, not honourable. And if the Home Front did not continue to think of its part in the war as noble and honourable, then the nation would not be able to carry on.

The first duty of the noble and the honourable in war is not to talk of the maimed or the dead. The injured or the fallen, yes, but not the maimed or the dead. Destruction was something that happened to buildings not humans. What happened to buildings could be seen to be terrible. What happened to bodies could not be seen and was nobody's business. You could print numbers, but not pictures. As for war artists, heroic men with head bandages were permissible; unheroic torsos without heads were out. Brush's vision was very much against the spirit of war, or how the nation wanted to countenance it.

Mr Feber knew what Brush was about, and Mr Feber knew from personal experience that what he was painting was valid and how he was painting it was exciting. Brush had found his subject; he had gone through the veil and beyond the kettles and apples. Mr Feber knew he had to be allowed to go on, even if he had to be hidden away while doing it.

Mr Feber knew too that newspaper pictures only ever show the machinery and the architecture, the devastation and the debris, the smoke and the rubble of war. Never the human beings beneath. But they were there, had to be; he himself had had first-hand experience, and he was quietly horrified and touched that this inexperienced pupil should display such extraordinary insight and imagination. Maybe he was witnessing what true art is about! Had Brush's subject matter only been something else – like the apples and kettles of old – then Mr Feber would have been able to proclaim him as a true talent. But Brush's images were war, the war outside the published photographs and the public policy, and they had to be hidden away.

So, while the headmaster and the rest of staff and his mother and the local doctor were all informed of Brush's 'condition', rather than create a scene and bring unwanted publicity to the school, Brush was allowed to continue his artistic crusade – in private.

'You finished then?' the corporal spoke quietly, reverentially, as if sensing he was in the presence of some higher talent.

'Nope,' said Brush, 'not quite.'

The corporal had watched Brush covering pages of drawings of the macabre triad before him and the pile of Bren carriers in the distance. And he had watched petrified as he stood up and went close in to circle the three men and concentrate on the details of their destruction, committing his scrutiny to many minor sketches. The corporal remembered how at school they had been taught to draw leaves in autumn, concentrating on the veins and minute gradations of light and shade in the colourings. Transfixed, he watched this young man do the same, bravely, professionally, dispassionately, as unaffected by his subject as an artist drawing a still life of a bowl of cherries.

Brush stopped abruptly and began packing away his sketch pad, charcoal and crayons.

'Now?' asked the corporal, rising, aching.

But Brush picked up his rifle silently and started to walk off down the hill in the direction of the mess of Brens. The corporal was not only lost for words, he

was devoid of even a simple expletive. As he opened
his mouth to try to form something, anything, Brush
paused on the path through the bushes and turned back
to the still-rooted corporal. 'By the way,' he called, 'don't
touch anything until I get back. I might need that model
again.' The corporal remained silent.

So Brush was given his own little room, no more than
a broom cupboard annex to the art classroom where
Mr Feber usually stacked all his materials. For twenty
years, since he returned from France in 1919 and took
up his post as assistant arts master 'with responsi-
bilities for outdoor sessions', he had had to squeeze
them into this ridiculously tiny room together with
the stock of collapsible chairs and easels, but nothing
had happened as a result of his constant pleading for
more space until Brush turned up with his 'condition'
and 'problem'; and then suddenly there was room all
over the school for Feber's 'blessed materials' because
Brush had to be accommodated in the box-room, like
a monster too hideous for public eyes. And in there
he perpetrated all his treachery and prepared for his
war.

Each day he was allowed to bring his newspapers and
magazines to school and deposit them in the box-room,
and whenever possible to devote extra time to drawing
and painting the other side of war. And in this cramped
retreat he fetched from his seething brain the gruesome
black and white and glorious technicolour images of
war that flashed across the screen at the back of his
mind and transmuted them to art paper, sketch pads,
notebooks, exercise books, backs of envelopes, inside
covers, newspaper margins, cardboard boxes, brown
paper shopping bags, and anything which surrendered
an unlikely square inch of blank in this frugal age of
rationing and shortages – whatever he could get his

brush or pen into. And in that way he depicted his war – the subtext of acceptable war.

Each day, the newspapers and boys' magazines of the time carried vivid photographs of the progress of the Nazis, from Warsaw to Paris and Dunkirk, across the desert to Alamein and back to Sicily, Anzio and Cassino, and on to the gates of Stalingrad and back, in the air and on the sea, convoys and U-boats, dive-bombers and fighters, London and Liverpool, Czechoslovakia and Greece, Belgium and Benghazi. Cameramen, photographers and artists, backed by war correspondents, reporters, and wireless commentators, all witnessed and conspired to chronicle the progress of war: the destruction, the devastation, the numbers. But no one ever revealed, to Brush or anyone else, the hidden account, the unmentioned toll. It was as if the world looked upon war as an experience that was totally impersonal, that took place between weapons, aircraft and tanks, U-boats and ships, landing craft and guns, jeeps and Bren-gun carriers – and above all between bombs and buildings. The second greatest conflict of modern times had nothing to do with blood, and the hordes of commentators who witnessed it found nothing to convey but 'destruction'. Numbers, yes. Casualties, certainly. Dead, reluctantly. Wounded, unfortunately. But they were details hastily passed by on the way through to assessment and statistics. 'Casualties' in whatever form had nothing to do with death, dying, wounds or pain. How *many*, yes; but *how*, no.

Brush had a mission. He knew they were hiding the truth and he went to the only place he knew to find it – his imagination. He had been operating behind his mind's eye ever since he could hold a crayon or wield a brush, but always giving up in the middle and 'smudging everything', not because he was trying to emulate the impressionists but because his mind refused to focus on what was in there. Until he saw the pictures from

Warsaw and suddenly the lens flicked into sharpness and focused in on the subject behind the veil. And for five years of school he fetched forth the images that came to him as he studied the newspapers, pored over the photographs, scanned the magazines, absorbed the wireless programmes, stared at the screens, and listened – to the unending *talk* of war.

Brush painted the subject of war. And added the blood. Each impersonal picture he brought to his monk's cell he matched with his impression, his view, his knowledge, of the other side, of what lay behind the impersonal designs of aircraft and bombs and blasts and crumbling buildings and mounting rubble. He went behind the patterns and painted the dead and the dying, the wounded and the suffering, the emaciated and the torn; screaming soldiers, wailing women, terror-struck children, slaughtered animals; arms, legs, heads, guts, eyes, muscles, the language of torn flesh and abused frames: the images of God men were rending asunder.

Because they thought him disturbed, they hid him away in his room. He committed all his violence to paper, so they were spared the embarrassment of having a pupil who was both deranged by war and disloyal to the war effort. The horror quickly turned to sympathy, from 'that maniac Morgan' to 'poor old Brush'.

It suited Brush. He was excused everything, in the name of peace and respectability. He spent his war doing exactly what he wanted to do, while all around him the nation fussed and flapped and became involved in the conflict raging outside.

From Hill 62 at Caen Brush set off down the track towards the second part of his theme, the stacked up Bren-gun carriers. And when he reached them he wandered around oblivious to the rush and tumble and roar of war about him: the turbulent movement of tanks and trucks and foot soldiers, bicycles and motor cycles, and the whole armour of war. Quietly, professionally, he surveyed the pile from all angles, squinting at the hesitant sun and raising his pencil to measure the model. After a good ten minutes of avoiding tanks and troops, he found a spot from which he could render the best representation and he squatted down. He sketched for a good hour while the sun struggled to awake after a hard slog the previous day; the great armies of the Allies shook the dust and sleep from their bodies; the tanks and trucks aroused themselves; and the whole circus of war retched and cleared its thick throat and once more wrenched itself into activity.

Heedless of it all, Brush sat and prepared his sketches: general views, closer sections, minute details, just as he had done with the three bodies. His coverage was intimate, total, rounded, and he filled page after page until he completed his pad. His comprehensive coverage of his first day of war was like a comprehensive coverage of all war, the whole four years of the eternity of war. Brush felt he could go home now.

No one ever died or was wounded in this war. Each time Brush saw another impersonal picture, and they were all impersonal, his imagination told him this could not be true. The pictures came to him as if the newspaper images were double thick and all he had to do was peel away the top layer and reveal the destruction underneath.

'Well,' he said when challenged, 'that's how *you* see it,' and he pointed to the magazine pictures of impersonal destruction, 'and that's how *I* see it. The only way I can describe it is to imagine what it would be like if these bombs were falling on us, here, right down in this classroom.' And he stabbed the brush to the floor because he always shook his brush vigorously before applying it to the paper, and the water splashed over the floor and desk and the other children watching.

He said to the snotty kids gaping open-mouthed, 'Bet you'd look a lot messier than my paintings.'

'Now, now, Morgan,' Mr Feber said for the benefit of the rules, 'don't overdo it, now.'

'How can I overdo it, Mister Feber?' asked the shocked Brush. 'Seems to me I can only *under* do it.'

Brush rose, stretched and walked across to the ruin of a house opposite. He pushed his way in past the hanging door and stepped over the rubble on the threshold. He found the remnants of a chair and settled down to glance through his pad.

They were the disturbed ones back home, refusing to acknowledge the logic of his work. He had believed that if he came and depicted what he saw in front of him they would finally be convinced that he wasn't deranged. He would show them the living – or dying – proof from the real Front instead of the unreal newspapers of home. And his mission would be accomplished.

Outside the activity hotted up as the morning progressed, but he sat on unaware that it had anything to do with him. He had done his bit, and fully intended to send home his pad 'as proof'.

They would prove the underside of war and when people saw war in all its raw disgrace they would abandon the conflict once and for all and beat their swords back into ploughshares.

He studied his pad. Now it was accomplished.

It never crossed his mind that these new pictures looked exactly like the ones he had been painting for years. And that the people back home might never notice the difference.

He heard a croak nearby and rose to look into the next

room. A soldier lay jack-knifed around a clutch of masonry as if hugging his beloved. But the movement had ceased.

Brush gazed at the scene and flicked through his pad. It was full, except for the clean inside back cover. With a full pad from the first morning he thought he had probably cracked it anyway, done enough at least to start to convince them. But he shrugged and fumbled for his charcoal. As he raised it the figure moved and life flowed back into the rubble. And with it the sounds of war outside.

He turned quickly, dropped his pad on the chair next door and picked up his rifle. Through the steaming rubble that once surrounded a window he saw an armoured truck making its way down from Hill 62 with troops from his own section standing in the back, their rifles sweeping the devastation around them for fear of lingering snipers or heroic left-over Germans. He stepped out over the threshold to signal for help holding his rifle high to clear the fractured masonry and signal the truck. The oncoming driver saw only the rifle emerging from the rubble and he swerved as two shots from the back rang out the second Brush's frame emerged and, as in one movement, pitched on to the street.

They found his pad on the chair and the lance-corporal in charge of the detail thumbed through it.

'Cor,' he said, 'what's this one been up to?'

'Bloody horrible, i'n it?'

Carrying the pack and pad outside the building the lance stopped and said, 'Reckon we should send it back with his gear?'

'Give his folks the creeps, that will. We gotta tell 'em he was a hero.'

The lance-corporal turned and tossed the pad through the shattered door of the piled up Bren carriers.

'War does funny things to blokes,' he said.

FRENCH LESSONS

Paris, 26th August 1944

Three

Buck Rogers went to war because he wanted to see Paris, to march down – 'or even up, I don't mind' – the Champs-Elysées to the Arc de Triomphe and the Tomb of the Unknown Soldier, to the cheers of screaming, rejoicing, ecstatic Parisian women and children – 'and men too if they want' – and to be hailed as their liberator.

Buck waited until he had got as far south as the Falaise Gap with the Second British Army and then decided to desert. He didn't really think of it as desertion. He wasn't exactly being a coward; he was only trying to get ahead of the rest. But he knew the authorities wouldn't look at it that way. When his unit reached Flers on Wednesday 16th August he knew it was time to go. He would have to make a break tonight if he were to have any chance of reaching Paris in time to liberate it before the Americans and the Free French themselves got there.

Buck's obsession started in September 1939 when he was evacuated from the Isle of Dogs to the Cotswold village of Dere and entered his first French class with Miss Mitchell – or was it Michel? Whatever, it was *Miss*. The first thing he saw on Miss Mitchell's wall was a map of Paris: a huge, brightly coloured expanse of geography that stretched from wall to wall decorated with all the outstanding places of interest – theatres, galleries, tombs, churches, palaces, restaurants – like an illuminated manuscript. And the second thing he saw was Miss Mitchell's bosom.

It wasn't only the *sight* of Miss Mitchell's map, it was the sounds she produced to go with it. By the time he was called up Buck had *heard* Paris as much as he had seen it, through her records of songs, street cries, markets, traffic, cabarets, river boats, street vendors, cafés and *gares* – nord *and* sud – and the clip-clop of horses and cabs. Above all, cabs.

One day that President or General chappie or whatever – that de Gaulle bloke – would step up to salute him and shake his hand and say 'Merci, Buck' or even 'Merci, Monsieur Rogers' and he would be able to say in return 'Ça ne fait rien' – it was nothing, mate – and in French of course, easily, nonchalantly, *avec aplombe*, because he had applied himself with alarming passion and devotion over four years to the French lingo – and the French teacher. So much so that the last thing he ever wanted to do was lose them by going to war; but when the time came he went willingly and knew exactly why.

The fighting had been rough enough since D-Day and Buck badly needed a breather, but that wasn't the reason he went now. He knew from what little intelligence he could glean from the rumours that Bradley's Americans were going hard for Paris and that the French Second Armoured Division were ahead at Alençon and were already smelling the coffee and croissants in Paris. If he had any chance of getting there to join in the liberation, however symbolic it was going to be, he would have to move. If he did it the right way, the official way, i.e. with his unit, he'd never make it. The British would certainly not be first and it was unlikely they would get there at all. The Yanks and the Frogs would have that opportunity, so he had no choice – he would have to join one of them.

Buck hadn't really meant to go to war at all. Had he been eighteen in 1939 he would have gone with all the others because it was the thing to do. But he was barely fourteen then and left to himself to get on with growing up, so that by the time 1944 came along and he was eligible he had got rather bored with war and rather pleased with his life in the Cotswold cottage. And Miss Mitchell.

He entered his first French class in September 1939. There weren't any male teachers left because they had all been called up. Suddenly overnight the school was run by women teachers and two elderly men – the headmaster and the janitor.

Evacuation had been a terrible wrench. Traumatic, it was, to be torn from the bosom of his family, but Buck's mother was rather a scraggy lass so he never really understood the expression 'bosom' anyway or had had first-hand experience of one that would encompass him and his three brothers and four sisters.

But once down in the Cotswolds he had found the perfect substitute. His first revelation was not the air, the fields or the freedom but Miss Mitchell's bosom, and he had stuck hard at French because she was the nearest he had come to being in love and the nearest he had come to sensing what kind of bosom might be ample enough to embrace him, if not the rest of his family too.

Buck had it worked out. Whoever was involved in the fighting to recapture the city itself, the French would certainly be allowed the final victory entrance. Diplomacy. The Yanks would almost certainly be there first. They were well ahead and had the power, but they would push on and surround the city and let the French have their day. Diplomacy.

He had no choice – somewhere along the route he would have to join the French, Leclerc's Second Armoured Division, and he'd have to do it before they got too far in front of him. If he could somehow get ahead and join them at the last minute, he might pull it off. During the uproar and pandemonium of fighting and celebration of the last few miles he might not be noticed because his French was improving by the hour and there would be too much happening and too much noise for anyone to pay him attention.

Once he had made his mind up, once he had taken the decision, Buck was ready, willing and most able to cheat, lie and dissemble, and engage in any shape or form of subterfuge or deception to realise his dream. He owed it to Miss Mitchell.

He would have to catch them up or overtake them a few miles from the gates of Paris. And there was only one way to do it – bicycle.

It took Buck some time to grasp that the painting on Miss Mitchell's wall was the map of a city. It seemed like the map of a whole country. Or even of a wonderland or promised land. It didn't seem to have anything to do with the congested streets and buses and tram cars and horses of his own world. To him cities were places of closely packed houses and dirty steets and horses fouling and tram cars grinding and noise and two vast football grounds that erupted every Saturday.

Up there on the wall was another world, this time a fairy tale. And yet as the hours and days dragged on between tedious classes of English and History and Geography and Maths and Science until French and Miss Mitchell and her map came around again, Buck came more and more to accept that this gorgeous painting was indeed the representation of a real place that existed and existed not so many moons away, although now in a land overrun by the forces of evil, the same forces of evil his own father was out there fighting, although the cities he was visiting on his war travels seemed mostly made of sand. And it troubled Buck sorely to hear that any day now France might fall, from where he could not fathom, but presumably from its pinnacle up there in the clouds above the Eiffel Tower, and with it its fair capital city the image of which graced Miss Mitchell's wall and brightened his days.

And Miss Mitchell brought the map alive. To her, teaching French was teaching about a people and a culture. Not for her the tedious world of learning long lists of dry words and phrases and converting them to black blotches on substandard wartime paper, only for her to cover in more red blotches. She ran her class like a French family and created miniature dramas of everyday life and situations in the home, school and market, shop, train and bus, observing high days and holidays, and binding it all together with a constant dash of poetry and splash of music, so that to cross the threshold into Miss Mitchell's room was to enter yet another separate world, a far cry from the Cotswolds and an even more distant scream from Manchester Street, Isle of Dogs.

The peace of the Cotswolds took away much of the pain of separation from his home and family; the haven of Miss Mitchell's classroom took away much more; and the expanse of her bosom obliterated whatever was left.

It had been too easy. Buck had simply waited until early evening and then walked away from his unit into a field with a stick in his hand as if he were going to do something very specific and would be back in a few minutes. He did it so casually, no one lifted a head or raised an eyebrow. All the way across the field he waited for the shout or the shot because he had no real idea where he was or was going, only a direction.

But neither shout nor shot came and he found himself climbing a fence at the far side, looking left to right on a farm road, crossing over, jumping the next ditch and climbing the next fence into another field. And so it went on.

Buck simply walked away from his war. And kept walking. It got dimmer and dimmer and by the time darkness was all around him he had made it to a group of farm buildings, but not even a dog barked and he slipped into a barn through a creaky door and flopped on a pile of sacks and dropped off to sleep.

When he awoke in the morning a young woman was looking down at him and asking in French if he wanted coffee. He got up, stretched, thanked her and followed her out into the fresh air but saw no signs of army of any kind and he wondered how this place could have stood so abandoned, so isolated, so by-passed.

At the door he signalled to her that he had to go around the back first and she nodded and went in and as he walked behind the building half expecting to find someone lurking with a gun, the smell of coffee came to him and woke him up and, although he was not a coffee drinker at all, he knew he would not refuse.

When he sat down she poured the coffee and asked him if he was a deserter and he shrugged and said in his faltering French 'half and half'. She asked him where he hoped to go and he said 'Paris' and she smiled and made a funny flick with her head as if to say 'nice place if you can get it, so drink up and good luck'.

He sipped his coffee and found it foul but it was hot and he smiled and nodded his thanks and asked her if she had a bicycle by any chance and she nodded and said 'yes'. He sipped more coffee and forced his wince into another smile and asked if he could borrow it. 'Borrow?' she asked. 'For Paris?' And Buck winced again and hung his head and said it was very important and she said that wasn't the point, it was a long way and how long did he have? He said five or six days, and she said that meant four or five because he should wait at least another day to get ready because he couldn't ride like that anyway, pointing to his uniform, and the area was seething with troops even if they were rather isolated here.

So he thanked her again and lay down on her sofa knowing it would all work out.

Miss Mitchell had many songs to go with her map: 'Auprès de ma blonde', 'Il était une bergère', 'Sur le pont d'Avignon'. But the *pièce de résistance*, the *chef d'oeuvre*, the *spécialité de la maison*, was Jean Sablon's *Le Fiacre*, the story about the horse cab clip-clopping its way through the busy streets. That sound above all transported Buck – in more ways than one – to the city on the wall.

At first when he had studied the golden map of the Paris Paradise he had gazed in awe at its colours, its formation, its highlights, its exquisite design with its long wide boulevards and its lined avenues of trees and its concentration around specific instances of grand architecture. He would stare and imagine what it would be like to be there, to walk past these cafés and restaurants and climb to the top of the Eiffel Tower to gaze down upon the wondrous design below. But, however much he animated it in his imagination, he only *saw* it – 'like one sees a silent movie'.

But once each lesson Miss Mitchell would fetch her gramophone from the cupboard and, very carefully turning a record over in her hand like some precious gift she had once been given by a lover – well, friend; she was after all *Miss* Mitchell – she would place it on the turntable, gently wind up the handle and play the songs of France, and Buck would drift off into dreams of broad boulevards and ample bosoms.

*   *   *

She begged him to stay when the news came on her wireless that fighting was severe at Falaise and that the Germans would not be yielding up Paris without a fight.

'You will never get through.'

'It will ease off. We have too powerful forces.'

'But you will not be able just to cycle through them.'

'I have to go south,' he said in a simple predestined way, as if he were a programmed migration bird.

'Orders?' she asked.

'In a way.'

'But you said you were a deserter!'

'They are still orders,' Buck said weakly.

'What good are orders at a time like this?' she asked.

Buck thought her very wise for a young woman, not much older than himself. But she had obviously been brought up in a tough place, with war on her doorstep for five years. Tougher than the Cotswolds.

'Maybe this is the time when it's most important to carry them out,' he tried limply.

'Rubbish! There isn't anyone left to give them!'

He wondered why it was still so quiet and no one had come home yet. Husband or father from work, children from school, mother from wherever. Maybe there weren't any.

Buck stopped being interested in war early one morning in May 1940 – Tuesday the eleventh in fact – when they announced that a man called Churchill had become prime minister. The news made his new parents very happy but he was far more interested in the sunshine and blossom and he slipped out after breakfast to play around in the great orchard before going off to school.

He had clambered up a large rogue woodland fir and was working his way from branch to branch when he suddenly found himself with his legs clutched around a thick branch and falling back down and over like a trapeze artist with his arms outstretched, looking upside down at the world and the blood rushing to his head. But at the same time as the blood came rushing to his head something else came rushing to his thighs and he swung there transfixed wondering what this extraordinary world would have to offer him next, what with all the trees and birds and the air and the attic room at the top which was his own and no other kids demanding a share in his corner of life, and girls giving him pangs of something he could not understand but it seemed to have to do with the time of year and just the joy of being in the open space of the Cotswolds.

But as he swung there he knew something else had happened to him, to his body. Something was cascading through his veins and engulfing his body but he couldn't pull himself up to investigate because he was scared the sensation would disappear and he would be left as he was often left these days fumbling and wondering with no one else to talk to: no mam, but she would not have told him anything anyway, and no dad, because he was out in the desert somewhere and for all he knew even dead by now, judging by all the casualties that kept getting reported in the papers and on the wireless. Besides, he had been away from them for so long they were just names now. He couldn't really feel and touch and smell them like he could the Hewitts and in particular Miss Mitchell and the girls in his class who more and more every morning were making his day a joy just by being there, and that what he was feeling now was all to do with them because it gave him the same kind of glow, except this time it was much stronger, flowing through him like warm water as if he was having a bath inside his body and he hung there trying to find ways to describe it. It was a kind of singing, really, but it didn't come from his throat. It came from his whole body. It vibrated around

him and he wanted to hang there forever and not let it
go because he had found something he might never ever
have found in his older life and he knew then that, when
the time came for him to go to war, he would find a way
out because there was no earthly or godly reason for him
to go and risk losing what he had found.

But he did not reckon on Miss Mitchell.

'No, I am a widow.'

It was late afternoon and no one had arrived. But they
could hear the guns in the distance.

God, he thought, 'she's not much older than me!'

'Oh, it's all right.' She came to his rescue. 'It was nearly
three years ago.'

God, he thought, 'she must have been a child bride!'
She had all the reasons not to go to war that he had
worked out back home, but she had had no choice. It
had been all war here. He looked up from his glass of
wine and she read in his disbelief that he was calculating
how young.

'I'm twenty-three.'

'The Germans?' he asked.

'In a way. Pneumonia! We couldn't get the vaccine.'
What a bloody stupid thing to die of!

On a dull Tuesday morning in June 1940 when Buck had
been away from home for eight months and was well
embarked on his new life of wide fields and illuminated
maps and ample bosoms, the news came that Paris had
fallen and the Hewitt's paper carried a cartoon of the
undying flame at the tomb of the Unknown Soldier
in Paris.

Buck went off to school with the heavy heart of
someone who has lost a friend he has never really
met yet – like being told your favourite pen pal from
Australia whom you had written to for years has died

and you wouldn't be able to meet him even for the first time.

Miss Mitchell said prayers, recited the Lord's Prayer in French, and they all stood with bowed heads and prayed that everything would be all right one day and the streets of Paris would begin to move again and the lifts in the Eiffel Tower would rise and the wind blow through the trees in the boulevards and the music of theatres and cabarets would start up again like a carousel at the village fair after a long winter.

Then she fetched her gramophone from the cupboard and very carefully, turning it over in her hand like some precious gift, she placed a record on the turntable and wound up the handle. She placed the needle in the groove and the scratching called the class to attention and they waited in silence to hear another hymn. But instead, floating up from the beaten grooves, came the clear tones of Jean Sablon fighting his way through the hiss and dragging his horse and cab into their classroom:

> *Un fiacre allait trottinant*
> *Cahin, caha,*
> *Hu', dia! Hop la!*

Le Fiacre – the very sound of Paris itself.

One solitary diamond winked feebly down at him through a distant stretch of teased muslin. It looked left-over, abandoned and he wondered if it had lingered because of laziness, or if the other night revellers had just sloped off when dawn came and left it hanging there. The thought of her broke his dream and he saw her standing there.

He closed his eyes and, like that morning in the orchard, everything came rushing but the words, and as he went under he heard a voice crying in his mind

how could he be unfaithful to Miss Mitchell and why
the fuck couldn't he be faithful to both, was the world
so bloody mean?

'I often lie watching the stars,' she said. And he
couldn't take his eyes from the muslin star winking
feebly but meaningfully through the soft filter.

Buck stayed behind at lunchtime to lie stretched out
along two benches at the back of the class and stare
up at the map of Paris and ponder the mystery of what
was happening to the world and his body.

Miss Mitchell came in and closed the door, unaware
that he was there. She took the record from her desk
again and carefully, reverently, placed the needle in
the groove and once again out of the silence came the
evocative, caressing tones of Jean Sablon floating up from
their beaten grooves, fighting their way through the hiss
and dragging the *Fiacre* and its obedient horse into the
classroom:

> *Un fiacre allait trottinant*
> *Jaune, avec un cocher blanc.*

Le Fiacre – the sound of Paris, and France.

Suddenly, in a flash and a crackle, Miss Mitchell and
Jean Sablon were together resurrecting Paris, making the
silent map on the wall into a movie with sound: giving
the plan of Paris Paradise a musical track.

Hitherto, the record of *Le Fiacre* was only one in her
collection. Now it was something special – the sound of
a whole city itself. Buck was about to leap up. But as he
turned, through gaps in the desks, he caught the tears on
Miss Mitchell's eye – it *was* Miss – and between the glisten
and the crackle, he saw Miss Mitchell and someone
struggling to resurrect Paris. But not Jean Sablon.

And in that moment Buck knew that Paris would
survive and that he would be there to help.

He lay rigid and silent and unbreathing, as the music of *Le Fiacre* lifted off from the turntable and moved across the classroom to hover over him and descend and wrap itself around him.

He struggled to find a way to compare it, an equivalent like the poets, and he gripped his body tight around the bench, straining to hold his breath. And the sensation came back to him from the time he had hung down from the tree in the orchard garden, and again he felt his body singing from the voice in his groin. It was the same for him now, but Miss Mitchell's tears were not for him or Paris, or the music, or Jean Sablon.

'You can use this.'

With one hand she placed the coffee beside him on the bedside table and gave the envelope with the other. The late afternoon sun strained through the curtains and cast shadows over her face that made her eyes look like black pits.

'It might keep you alive.' She turned away, gathered her clothes from the chair on the other side of the bed and left the room.

Bordi. Male. 15th January 1919.

She had given him her husband's birth certificate, a sturdy piece of parchment, brown-creased at the folds, its copperplate blinking dazzled in the unfamiliar sun.

Christian name: Armand. 14th February 1919.

And the christening certificate, giving the boy his name. Twenty-five years later giving another boy his chance.

'And these.'

She came back into the room fully dressed.

'You are about the same size.'

Over her arm she carried a coathanger with a man's

trousers and jacket. She laid them gently on the bed, together with a shirt and socks.

From early on Buck thought he would find a way out of going to war when his time came, because he was far too busy growing up to bother about war.

'God, it don't half get on your wick, don't it?' he often said to the Hewitts who were much more heroic about it than he was. And until that lunchtime revelation all he had really wanted to do was concentrate on Miss Mitchell's bosom and sundry related sensations.

He resented most that no one ever said anything about the pains of growing up and only waiting to go to war. Nothing but talk of the greater glory of everyone going off to serve and sacrifice. Never any thought that a bloke going into puberty around 1939 had other things on his mind. He may hide himself behind war comics and magazines but his real mind was elsewhere, and it wasn't the dunes of Benghazi or the beaches of Sicily either, *or* the nooks and crannies of battlefields from Dunkirk to Alamein. He was interested in other nooks and crannies.

The one thing uppermost in Buck's mind was not the heroics of desert rats but the upheaval going on in his own body and having to contemplate throwing it away on some forlorn foreign field before he had had a chance to explore and express what it was all about.

And then there was Miss Mitchell.

He felt like a gypsy now.

Stretched out on a haystack contemplating the heavens, dressed in the rough serge of a dead French peasant, false birth certificate, forged identity card, masquerading under the name of Armand Bordi – a vagabond making his own way in his own time from a farm near Flers to Paris. By bicycle.

And all around him the world at war.

He watched the soldiers on the horizon. A shimmer of heat hung in front of them like a veil rustling in the morning breeze. They seemed very far away, very private. The curtain that separated them heightened his sense of himself as an intruder, a peeping Tom.

It looked like a caravan grouped around a desert oasis. Men seemed to walk in slow motion, as if burdened by the heat of packs and boots and helmets. Well, it was August.

It was all too unreal. As unreal as the gypsy on the haystack. Any moment now he would slide off the stack, re-mount his borrowed bicycle and carry on with the long ride to Paris. Three days? Four?

When the time came he volunteered early. Cheated his age. With the help of the local councillor responsible for the chores of the community, like registering births and marriages and deaths. Buck was straight with him. The war was nearing its close. Paris might soon be liberated. He had to be there. It was his right to liberate it. His alone. He had this mission. This was *his* war. If he didn't go now, he might arrive too late. If he waited until it was exactly his time, he might miss it. Others would do the job. Paris would never be the same without his liberating contribution even if others did liberate it.

'But I thought you were one of . . .'

But now it was different. Now he had found his reason. He would not be going blindly to war. He would be going deliberately to Paris to liberate it from those Germans who had captured it and cut down all the trees you could have experiences on and destroyed whatever it was that made Miss Mitchell hang upside down in tears in a Paris garden playing *Le Fiacre*. He had to help to bring it back to her, despite the pain of realising she had experienced it all without him. Or maybe because of.

She had felt her own sensations somewhere else and with . . . so she must have . . . maybe had . . . could have had . . . probably did . . . almost certainly might . . . and the blood of jealousy rushed to his head and he gripped hard and thought how stupid he had never thought that she could have had these same sensations with someone else or because of someone else, and that she was not waiting for him to grow up and climb down from his tree, not preserving her bosom for him until he was ready. She had had her own . . .

And in the same moment the rush surged over him and he wanted to cry out in despair it began to subside, because the music was soothing too; and he came out of his coma like he had had to climb down from that tree, and he wanted to do things for her. Maybe growing up was about that – or that too. In a flash he had gone through three or four changes to his body and mind and he now knew that he would go off to war not just to free Paris – but that too.

He turned over slowly to lie on his front. Sharp needles of dried grass scratched his hands and face. The rough thread of his trousers scratched the inside of his thigh. The leather patches on his sleeves creaked – and he chilled. The sound rasping against his spine, no doubt.

The French troops were regrouping. They were nearly there now. Again the guns thundered and he was near enough to hear the cries and the voices. He lifted his head from the tangle of hay and saw figures like black puppets dancing on the horizon – a shimmer of trucks, tents and steel-helmeted soldiers, but this time in the heat of the guns not August. And the horizon was no further away than the end of the field in which his haystack stood. A thousand yards? Less. It wasn't the leather that had grated. For the first time since he was a schoolboy in the Cotswolds he felt fear.

His eyes narrowed even more. The nearer strands of grass blurred. The figures on the horizon continued their weird, pantomime motions.

A few days ago he would have viewed them for what they were – troop movements. Tonight, yards from his goal, his body was charged by vibrations that echoed Cotswold trees and classrooms and French farms.

He stumbled over the field dragging his bike. It looked better. When he reached the other side, he dropped his bicycle and dragged one of the corpses into a bush and saw the insignia. He had met up with the Second Division at Rambouillet in the nick of time – 30 kilometres from Paris.

In the twilight he stripped the French soldier of his uniform and hitched a lift in a crowded truck. He kept his head down as if shattered. The following morning he was outside the Hotel Meurice in Paris.

General Leclerc had detailed Lieutenant Karcher to take command of five Sherman tanks and two hundred men and capture General von Choltitz, the German officer commanding Paris, inside the hotel, and force him to sign a surrender pact.

The men poured out of their trucks and down from the tanks and attacked the building. But the Germans had not yet said quits. They put up fierce opposition in the square even for that hopeless last ditch, because the fall of Paris was virtually over. Nevertheless it had to be done and seen to be done formally and that needed a few more lives to seal the victory. For a violent few minutes the square was ablaze with gunfire and shells and screams, and Karcher took his small force through the entrance to find von Choltitz in an upstairs room. They brought him out and rushed him to the *Police Préfecture* where Leclerc was waiting and the capitulation was signed.

In the square outside the Hotel Meurice, the French

gathered their dead and set about identifying them. There were problems. The ferocious resistance of the German garrison even at that late hour had weakened neither their resolve nor their fire-power. One of the casualties hardly looked French at all – crudely clad in an ill-fitting uniform as if unfamiliar with correct army dress. The officer-in-charge felt quite humble to see the kind of men who had been willing to fall so that the cabs in Paris would run again and the young would swing on its trees.

MESSERS' MODEL

Arnhem, September 1944

Four

On the way down to Arnhem, Messers Smith shouted across to his mate, 'I used to build bridges like that with my fretsaw.'

When they reached the ground Harvey Nichols pulled in his parachute and said, 'Well, we'll need more than a saw to get rid of this one.'

'Get rid of it!' said Messers. 'Is that what we're supposed to be doing?'

'No,' said Nichols, 'but I expect we'll end up destroying it whatever we're supposed to be doing. Nothing ever works out here like it's *supposed* to.'

After the long stalemate in Normandy during the summer of 1944 Messers Smith found himself part of the great allied scheme to sweep through France, Belgium and Holland, with the help of Patton's Third US Army, Montgomery's Twenty-first, and Harvey Nichols. But now, instead of bridgeheads, the problem they were facing was bridges pure and simple. They were all over the place, especially in the north, which wasn't surprising as the Low Countries seemed mostly water anyway.

In one way, the advantage lay with the Germans because, as they raced back to asylum behind the Siegfried Line and their own sacred Rhine itself, they

could hold up the Allied advance by destroying the
bridges behind them. In another, they were giving up
so much territory in the process they would soon be
fighting on their own soil.

'How long you been in then?' asked Messers, scrambling
over the airfield outside Arnhem trying to untangle the
mass of ropes stretching all the way to the wayward
parachute bobbing around like a teasing balloon.

'This mob?' asked Harvey. 'Couple of months, give
or take,' he said confidently, easily standing erect while
playing in his parachute strings like landing a docile
sardine.

'Ah, *well.*'

'What's a fretsaw anyway, Messers?' said Nichols as they
clambered into their battle gear shortly after breakfast
that Sunday morning. 'You fret away like a dog worrying
at a bone, do you?'

'No, no, not *that* fret!' Messers exclaimed as he tried to
concentrate on the clothing he had spread out on the floor
in front of him. Messers always had to see everything laid
out like a carpenter's tools before starting to dress and kit
himself. 'It's fret as in, well, fretwork.'

'Oh,' said Harvey, calmly studying Messers' antics.
'That's interesting.'

'Building my own world, I was.'

'So you said.'

Messers had been on about his fretwork model of his
'City for Tomorrow' since breakfast.

'Building it out of frets, then?' Harvey pressed on,
intrigued by the young man's meticulous habits. As a
seasoned soldier recently transferred to Airborne from
Special Ops, few military operations took him very
long.

'No, not out of frets, man, out of *wood*!'

'What's the fret bit then?'

'The fret bit,' said Messers, struggling into his suit, 'is the kind of patterns you make in the wood.'

'Ornamental, you mean?'

'Yes. Ornamental. Like wickerwork, only in wood instead of wicker.'

'What kind of things did you make, then? I mean, before the one about Utopia?'

'Oh, all sorts of things,' said Messers, wandering about the room, stomping and thumping, coaxing his gear to fall into place around his body. 'Galleons, liners, aircraft, cars . . .'

'For fun?'

'For a hobby, yes.'

'Sounds great.'

They both got up and made for the door.

'Bit like making stained glass,' added Messers, twitching as if something on him was the wrong size.

'Go on,' said Harvey, impressed, 'you make stained glass! What, for churches and cathedrals?'

'No, no,' said Messers at the entrance. 'I said it's *like* that. Like you have to make patterns out of lead, see, and then fit the glass bits in.'

'Never knew that.'

They emerged into the autumn air.

'Getting a nice day for it,' said Messers, waddling over the tarmac laden down with his heavy gear. 'I don't half welcome the fresh air after being cooped up in my workshop for so long.'

'Oh, this'll make a nice change for you, I'm sure,' said Harvey, casually striding out as if off to the beach.

Standing in the queue for the aircraft, Messers went on, 'With fretwork you use three plywood and cut out the patterns, the ornament bits, with a very fine saw like a needle with teeth down the side.'

'Sounds pretty delicate stuff.'

'Oh, it is, very. You have to be skilled and delicate with your work like a crotchet maker.'

Messers mounted the steps first and Harvey said over his shoulder, 'So how come you can do all that refined work and make such a hash of winding in your parachute every time?'

At the entrance, Messers paused and turned. 'That's different,' he shouted back. 'I'm not fully trained yet, am I?'

'Well,' said Harvey, 'hope it's not too late.'

Monty's way around the problem was to beat the Germans by leap-frogging them and dropping paratroopers in advance of the main army to hold the bridges until the supporting ground troops caught up. A simple enough idea but it depended on the most intricate coordination: getting divisions of men and equipment from various starting points in England and France to rendezvous together and on time and safely landed and linked up with other scattered units and ground forces and supply lines and all firmly connected through a perfected, reliable communications system. 'A fretwork job, really.'

And as part of this grand strategy Messers found himself detailed to take one of the three bridges over the Neder Rijn at a Dutch town called Arnhem. Although he didn't have to do it on his own, the task suited Messers perfectly because it exactly fitted his idea of 'a preserving war' rather than 'a destroying one', and he thought that if he could get there before the Germans and save the bridge for the main forces then not only would he have done his bit to please Monty, he would have preserved his sense of respect for the architecture of a place as well. So Messers shuffled up along the bench in his C-47 Dakota and clipped himself in and adjusted his bulging pack and gripped his gun and waited for the off, confident he wasn't embarking on a destruction exercise so much as a preservation one.

Prior to Arnhem the rest of the Airborne Division had had no fewer than seventeen previous operations planned and then cancelled since the Normandy landings and although it was all right by Messers because they had all been planned to destroy, the others were getting impatient. Messers was quite calm.

'So, how come you got mixed up in this lot if you're so good with your hands, Messers?' asked Harvey, buckling himself up and settling in for the flight as if ready for the air hostess to take his order. 'You'd think they'd find you something a bit more refined to play with than that bloody sten.'

The Dakota taxied off.

'Well, they never offered me anything else, did they. Said they were short.'

'You tell them about your fretting?'

'Not fretting, *fretwork*. Ooops!'

'We're airborne.'

'Oh, I wondered what the bump was.'

'Did you try telling them about your model for tomorrow?'

'They didn't seem to want to listen. I think they were a bit rushed the day I joined up. It was Wednesday, see.'

'Early closing?'

'Expect so.'

There were three bridges at Arnhem, a railway bridge to the north, a ship bridge which carried road traffic and could be floated apart to allow barges through, and the main road bridge to the south. When the Germans invaded in 1940 the Dutch destroyed the main bridge but the Germans had rebuilt it as they were obviously intent on staying. Messers knew there were three bridges but not which one he would be saving.

On the way across that morning, Harvey said, 'I often wondered what you kids were getting up to while us lot were out there defending your freedom and independence and the right to do fretwork.'

'Fretwork, mostly,' said Messers.

'I was about your age when I joined up in '39. Never got much time for hobbies. How did the idea come?'

'Well,' said Messers, fidgeting and adjusting his awkward gear, 'they were always telling us at school that we were fighting this war in order to build a better world fit for heroes to live in. So I used to think about how I'd like it to look. But it was me Mum really that put me on to the model.'

Messers had been doing fretwork since he was a kid. His father taught him until he went off to war in 1939 and then his brother took over when they learned Dad wouldn't be coming back from Alamein. Then Joe went off and didn't come back from Salerno so Messers was left on his own and had to set about teaching himself; 'to keep my mind off things'. He got stuck in, kept his head down and made Messerschmitts and Heinkels and Stukas and Spitfires and Hurricanes, 'a proper little private war' complete with airfield, anti-aircraft guns and hangars. He hung his pretty machines from the ceiling with thread like puppets, and his friends came around regularly to admire his work and see his shows.

For reasons she didn't explain, his mother preferred the German Messerschmitt fighter. 'What you on tonight, then,' she would ask, 'another squadron of Messers?'

Messers never understood that she might be goading him on, trying to get him to think of something else and turn his talents on to another tack. But his friends heard her say the same thing so often, they lumbered him with the name.

He worked at his models night and day and weekends and gave up football and cricket and stayed at home to keep his mother company and to work at getting the pain of his loss out of his system. But he was putting something back too, sawing away in the attic room night and day, instead of moping and grieving.

They landed at two o'clock on a Sunday afternoon in September eight miles west of a town called Arnhem, thousands of paratroopers floating down alongside Messers to an airfield already peppered with gliders carrying foot soldiers. Messers' unit was detailed to advance into the town immediately to take the bridges while the rest guarded the airfields.

'Told you,' said Nichols, calmly packing up his 'chute into a neat round ball and stuffing it into its bag, 'I should leave your fretsaw for when you get home again,' and he waited patiently while Messers struggled with the capricious silk as if grabbing a swarm of butterflies in a summer breeze.

'Anyway, why get mixed up in this? It's all about bringing worlds down.'

'Well, we'll have to build them up again, won't we?'

'Not me, mate. Once we've razed this little lot to the ground, I'm off. They can sort it out for themselves.'

'But they're not intending to destroy it *all*, otherwise why are they sending us?'

'C'mon,' said Harvey, looking around for transport. 'Looks as if our carriages haven't turned up yet. Fancy an eight mile stroll on a Sunday afternoon?'

The quiet landing suggested that the Brass had at last got it right and organised an operation that was destined to go 'according to plan'.

'Nice when you get to work with people that do their

homework proper for once, isn't it?' observed Harvey. 'I like that. My kind of boss.'

Harvey and Messers walked on enjoying their Sunday afternoon hike and trying to pronounce impossible names like Heelsum and Klingelbeekseweg and Roermondsplein.

'Might come in handy one day,' said Harvey. 'Do *you* do crosswords, Messers?'

'No,' said Messers, 'always far too busy with my fretsaw.'

'Course.'

Harvey and Messers pressed on. It wasn't an exciting district but it was peaceful and it was early autumn.

One afternoon Messers' mum climbed to the attic and walked around the floor pointedly studying all the aircraft and guns and hangars and airfields and tanks decorating the room to overflowing and finally broke her silence. 'Your dad and Jim were out there trying to build this better world they're all talking about and you're stuck in here with your war and machines.'

'What you on about?' Messers asked, rounding the corner on a Heinkel fuselage.

'Your dad didn't get much chance to build one out of sand dunes and Jim had less building one out of water, but at least they had the right idea.' And she looked all around as if searching for something she had come to fetch.

'Now, see what *you're* doing about it – building another bloody war.'

And she went back down.

When they reached the town the CO despatched one of the companies to take care of the first target, the railway bridge. Harvey and Messers waved them good luck and carried on.

'Quite a nice spot,' said Harvey, gazing around at the quiet Sunday afternoon houses. 'You'll enjoy rebuilding this.'

'Who said we're taking it down?'

'Everywhere we go and whatever we say we're doing, it's always a mess when we've done with it.'

They heard the sound of machine-gun fire behind them and across the river to the south from the direction of the railway bridge. 'C' Company must have come into action already.

Harvey gave a knowing shrug as if to say: *Well, it had to happen.*

Messers said, 'Not the kind of thing you do on a Sunday, is it?'

'Fight, you mean?' asked Harvey, striding on.

'Well, yes, that too. But anything really. It should be a day of rest. I only once worked on my model on a Sunday.'

More gunfire reached them from the bridge.

'Religion?' More gunfire. Crossfire now, coming at them as if chasing them on their way to the rendezvous. 'Or your mum?'

'More the *feeling.* There's something about Sunday.'

'Especially tea time.'

An enormous explosion halted them in their tracks and Harvey and Messers felt the vibrations come at them through their feet. Something had happened to the railway bridge.

A burst of gunfire tore through them from their left and in a flash they too were into action.

'Especially tea time,' shouted Harvey, on his stomach in the gutter.

Surrounded by all his models Messers sat in his room for an hour and a half doing nothing but ponder the universe. His mother came back with his tea and said, 'Don't be late now. School in the morning.'

When she had gone he sipped his tea and walked about studying each of his exquisitely carved machines. When his tea was finished he began to take everything apart. He didn't destroy any model, but broke up each into its component parts.

He worked on through the night carefully dismantling every replica, selecting the bits he could re-use and ditching the bits that were impossible, like sifting through rubble and saving the better bricks. By the time he turned in that night there was no trace of a gun or an aircraft or anything to remind one that the theme had been war. And in place of all the completed works there were piles of spare pieces of wood awaiting destruction or the next venture.

When he came home from school that afternoon he began to design his city.

Sheltering in a doorway of a house in Arnhem Messers said to Harvey, 'If I don't come back they'll have a plan to go on.'

Harvey said, 'I'm counting three and we dash for that line of cars. Right.'

'Right. It was coming on good when my papers arrived.'

'One . . . Two . . .'

'My mother's looking after it.'

'Three!'

Messers fought with his conscience over whether to join up or not, because the law said if a family had lost more than two of its members then any one else of eligible age didn't have to go. But he couldn't stand the thought and shame of being an able-bodied bloke that the folks who did not know would jeer at.

'A rum thing war,' said Harvey reloading. 'Gets you every which way.'

*   *   *

The CO detailed the second company to look after the intruders on the raised ground of Den Brink to the left and took Messers, Harvey and the rest from their shelter behind the cars to the road bridge. It was still a fair walk and they plodded on aware that the evening was drawing in. They sighted the ship bridge lying harmless enough and seemingly abandoned and pressed on through Eusebiusplein. Ahead of them in the near dusk stood the huge arched iron construction of the road bridge. Across it German transport was passing peacefully.

The CO signalled his company to halt and in the dying light invited them to take a few minutes to absorb the sight, to take a deep breath and feel the measure of what lay ahead of them.

'Looks solid enough,' sighed Harvey. 'Bit too solid for your fretsaw, Messers.'

'I told you, I didn't come all this way to do *damage*!'

'Right, that's our target, men. Let's go!'

The vicar said that maybe Messers should consider that he owed it to his mother to stay even if it did mean suffering the accusations of others.

'If I stay,' Messers told his mother, 'I could help where Dad and Jim would have helped.'

'For a year or two, yes. But you're nearly eighteen now and war or no war you won't be hanging around here much longer. You might be doing a lot to help me now but it couldn't last, see? Not in the nature of things.'

The pair of them sipped their tea.

'No,' she said. 'We'll have to think of another reason, I'm afraid.'

Messers, Harvey and Co. barricaded themselves into houses on the north side of the bridge. Other soldiers emerged from nowhere and crowded in with them.

A patrol set off to cross the bridge and take the other side but gunfire from the pill-box directly facing them at the approach repulsed them.

'You should have appealed, Messers,' said Harvey. 'Stuck to your fretwork and left us to get on with pulling this lot down. Then you could have had yourself a job to come home to when we've crossed this little bridge, see?'

His mother said, 'Well, all the other boys have to go, don't they? Like your dad and Jim.'

'They would have wanted me to stay – for your sake too.'

'Well, pain is pain is pain, isn't it? I can't say my grief is double because I lost Dad and Jim anymore than I could say it'd be treble if I lose you. It doesn't work like that.'

Another patrol set off. A German group tried to cross from the south side and were beaten back. Another party left to attack the pill-box. About four hundred troops were now assembled in houses and a school and anywhere they could find shelter on the north side and the battle had begun in earnest.

Guns blazed and ammunition roared madly to and fro across the bridge. Inside one of the houses Harvey took pot shots through slits and Messers squatted frightened but fascinated as his bridge held firm. On both sides men were killed and wounded.

Messers stared long and hard at the sections of his rough model. 'Will that do?' he asked.

His mother stared long and hard at the pieces, then said, 'Why not? Until it's finished.'

So Messers filled in his application for deferment and had it endorsed by the vicar and the papers arrived to tell him he didn't have to go. He didn't know whether to feel sad or pleased but he had done it and that was that and he folded the envelope with the short bit of paper and got down to the shopping arcade he was working on and kept his head down again and blotted out all thoughts of war and stigma.

Early on Monday morning the Germans wheeled armoured cars and half-tracks into position and closed on the buildings where Messers and Co. sheltered. The Germans attacked and were met with volleys of gunfire, grenades and mortars. They retired leaving behind piles of their dead, and wrecked vehicles.

Harvey was still in command of his peep-hole and seemed unflappable. Messers found his own and joined in but made sure all his firing was directed away from the bridge.

Then the Germans opened up with shells and mortars from the far side and the buildings started to crumble all around Messers and Harvey. Cannon and machine-gun fire ripped patterns of holes across the concrete at window level and left great gaping holes so that the men inside seemed to be caught behind a mesh of dust and concrete.

Messers could now see his bridge clearly and that it remained untouched.

Messers kept at his city of fretwork – his ornamental, patterned stained-glass City for Tomorrow with towering skyscraper flats and sprawling open hospitals scattered between green patches for the kids and glass houses for the elderly and large meandering shopping ways with separate shops strung along the route each looking different and individual as if the owners themselves had chosen the style and had done each in a separate intricate design of fretwork mosaic.

He never left his attic. His mother brought him tea and told him when lunch or supper was ready. She paid no attention to what he was doing.

Twice a week the vicar 'popped in' to ask how he was 'coming along' and to check if he needed more blades or joiner's pencils or books on architecture which he was able to borrow from the main library.

Outside the war was still raging. Inside Messers' peace was under construction.

At Arnhem communications with the outside world were not what they should have been for the troops on the north side of the bridge. Maybe the equipment was inadequate. Maybe the operators were thinning out. Maybe the concentrations of tall buildings didn't help. Whatever, little was getting into or out from the beleaguered force.

'Pity,' said Harvey, nestling down on his bed of bricks, 'I miss a good play in the evening.'

'Light?' asked Messers, cuddling up with his sten.

'No, Home Programme, me.'

The buildings were disintegrating all around them. Holes gaped, fires kept breaking out, ammunition was running down, water running out. Down in the cellars the groans of the growing crowd of wounded floated unhindered up through the tattered walls and wrecked floorboards.

'Not much point in staying inside soon,' said Harvey.

Looking around, Messers said, 'Can't think what's holding it together.'

'Like I told you,' said Harvey, 'you don't preserve anything in a war. Even if you think you've come to protect it, you only end up tearing it apart.'

Messers wet his finger and wiped the dust from the grooves of a grenade.

'Bridge is still holding,' he said.

*　　　*　　　*

'They've landed in Normandy,' said his mother, setting down his tea.

Messers flicked sawdust off a grocer's shop and said, 'That's about right, then.'

'Finished?' she asked.

'Near enough,' he answered, lifting his cup. The model had become the room, or the room the model. Streets, main roads, shopping ways, shops, houses, flats, hospitals – each a highly individual design stood separate and distinct as if carved out of tapestry. And it was in a way, because of the nature of fretwork; a city constructed out of patterns and designs, as if the intricate shapes of loops and curves and curls and sharp edges *were* the various buildings. They were woven into the patterns: the ornamentation predominated but did not stop the buildings performing their function. A fairyland too, yet solid in its delicateness, strong in its intricacy, defiant in its refinement.

'I can start the painting tomorrow,' he said. 'Should be finished by the weekend.'

'Destroying things is against my principles,' said Messers.

'I'd noticed,' said Harvey from his brick pillow.

'Just in case you thought it was all bull.'

'No, not at all. Only, don't tell the sergeant. He's touchy these days.'

'I was getting quite obsessed with all my objects,' Messers confessed. 'It was like my mind was up there in its own attic too.'

'You can get too intense about things,' Harvey observed. 'I know.'

'Treating them like icons, or holy relics, know what I mean?'

'It happens.'

'You ever get like that, Harvey?'

'Well, up to a point, but never about *your* kind of models.'

'You know,' Messers turned over to look at Harvey and whisper through the dust rising from his slightest movement. 'I was beginning to treat them as human. I was even *talking* to them. Can you believe that?'

'After four years in this mob, yeah.'

Another shell exploded and the plaster kept falling between them.

'Volunteering for airborne was not particularly smart, was it?' said Harvey dreamily.

'Well,' said Messers, 'it seemed different at the time.'

More gunfire raked their building and cries of pain rang out from the next room. Harvey turned over on his bricks and said, 'You got yourself a proper dilemma, haven't you, Messers? How to finish this war off and get back to your great City of Tomorrow project without destroying anything.'

'I was thinking just that as we floated down on Sunday. Then you pointed out that whatever we were dropping in to preserve, chances were we'd destroy it anyway.'

'The way of war, they say.'

'Hell bent on doing my bit for the war and getting it over and done with provided I didn't destroy anything! Imagine!'

'That's the thing about war. Plays hell with the logic.'

'Maybe I was too long in that attic.'

'Well, shouldn't think you'll be too long in this one.'

On Sunday evening Messers stood in the kitchen wiping the paint from his fingers with turpentine.

'We'll need to keep the windows open, otherwise we'll be poisoned. How did the vicar find paint like that during war time? Prayer?'

'Oh, no, the Good Lord would never listen.'
'Black magic?'
'Or market.'

First thing Tuesday morning the Germans fired a heavy anti-tank gun at the group of buildings in which Messers, Harvey and Co. were having an early breakfast. Harvey said that that probably wouldn't make things easier.

Messers peeped through the open roof to see the bridge still silently intact and a large party of Germans lining up outside with machine guns.

Someone dragged in a box of grenades and Messers, Harvey and Co. helped themselves and took up positions beside the open holes overlooking the bustling Germans fussily preparing their guns in the street below.

'Not much left for them to fuss about,' said Harvey.

'Or point,' added Messers.

They waited patiently until the Germans were all set to begin and then tossed their grenades and followed through with their Stens. Messers kept on firing and as the walls around him dropped away in large exhausted lumps of plaster he thought of the mess they were making for the poor owners who would come back one day.

The bridge still stood.

He came home on Monday lunchtime and said, 'I'll be off Wednesday.'

'No fuss about the application?'

'Weren't interested. Obviously need anyone they can get.'

'Did they tell you what to take?'

'I've got a list. Not much.'

'Give it over and I'll sort the things out.'

After they ran out of grenades and the Germans of men, the firing stopped and everyone left standing started to drag the wounded downstairs to place them alongside the others in the basement and to fetch the German wounded in from the street to join them.

At supper on Tuesday evening, he said, 'Mind you take the ladder away when it's dry. Don't want anyone else interfering.'

'Course.'

The Germans set fire to the house at the end of the row and it spread quickly. More fleeing troops crammed into the crumbling house with Messers, Harvey and the wounded.

In the afternoon an aircraft flew in and dropped bombs. But the keen pilot came so low he nicked his wingtip against the church spire and carried on down into the lake nearby. Everybody cheered.

Messers thought it should be over soon as everyone was a bit tired of it now and the bridge was still standing and there wasn't much ammunition left.

'Might have use for your fretsaw yet,' said Harvey.

'I told you I'm not here for *that*,' said Messers.

On Wednesday morning he came down from the attic and said, 'On second thoughts the ladder will need to stay. I shan't close the windows. They should stand open for a few days yet. Powerful stuff that.'

'Like his sermons.'

'When you're certain it's really dry, cover it with dust sheets. And if it's a really hot summer watch it doesn't get tacky.'

'Like I said, like his sermons.'

In the evening a Tiger Tank appeared and fired two 88 mm shells into what was left of the group of buildings and school. The following morning, Wednesday, more tanks turned up and continued the bombardment and some British Bren-gun carriers arrived but couldn't force their way through.

The sergeant said, 'We're making a dash for the bridge, you lot!' and Messers turned to see he was talking only to him and Harvey. During a rare lull they emerged from the rubble and made for the near spans where they fought hand to hand with Germans setting demolition charges.

At the station on Wednesday she said, 'I'm happy you finished it.'

'Well, I had to. Otherwise it would have preyed on my mind.'

'Well, now you can rest in peace.'

'Something like that.'

'Don't you think we've done enough now, Sergeant?' Messers said during a lull.

'Eh?'

'I'm getting to like these lulls.'

'Shut it, Messers. I'm busy.'

Messers pointed back up the road to the pulverised buildings and the spirals of steel and the coils of bodies strewn along the way.

'We should be here to build them instead, you know, Sergeant. That's what we're fighting for, isn't it?'

'What the fuck you on about?' said the sergeant.

'To build bridges. You know, between nations and all that.'

'Christ!' said the sergeant, glancing at Messers relaxing and Harvey smoking, then at the Germans regrouping, and finally burying his head in the muck. 'Not one of *them*! Of all the bleeding luck!'

Messers had his back to the bridge now, facing the Germans preparing to advance with more demolition charges.

'If there's one thing I can't stand,' the sergeant groaned,

lifting his head from the dirt, 'it's blokes wot got fucking visions.'

'Pay attention, now, Sergeant,' said Messers, soothingly. 'Here they come.'

FULL MILITARY HONOURS

Tilburg, October 1944

Five

Covering up the body of the German soldier somewhere in the no man's land of the Netherlands, Kingdom Cumming felt an extra shiver go down his spine because he had been through this once before when he was younger, much younger, although four years later it seemed twice that long. Only this time he knew there would be no double cover-up and he laughed at the pun as he drove the spade into the wet earth because the tension he was feeling with the grey lump at his feet was stretching right back to that freezing March morning when the three of them found the dead German pilot washed up on their beach and decided to bury him themselves because as children they were excluded from the war and they wanted to play their own part in it and be allowed for once to make rules of their own.

The war seemed to have got itself into a rut for Kingdom and Co., plodding drearily through flat sodden fields at a time of year and through a type of terrain more suitable for digging potatoes than performing heroics on. Big battles lay behind: Normandy, Caen, Falaise, and no doubt bigger ones lay ahead, unless the Germans suddenly decided to pack it in. But the way they had fought for every sod and ditch since D-Day, already four months behind, there didn't seem much hope of that.

Arnhem was behind as well of course, except that geographically it lay ahead, and still had to be taken. In these damp days of October '44 with another Christmas approaching and precious little sight of an end to it all, the effort at Arnhem seemed sadder every day. A bravado attempt to leap over the Germans and cut them off and shorten the war was the propaganda. It didn't seem that way now, more like one of those mad, Balaclava gestures that was going to look wonderful in the history books and every schoolboy's *Bumper Book of Bravery*, but not on a damp October morning in Holland. Or was it Belgium? Or Germany, even? Or maybe still France? That was the trouble: most things had lost their direction or focus; the map was blurred, and visibility in autumn plays tricks.

Kingdom slithered on the damp topsoil and closed his eyes and felt the ache in his arms and tension at the waist as he swung the shovel on its edge down into the earth and levered it to loosen the soil then drove it in and it stuck and lodged and he pulled so that the veins stood out all over his body and he wanted to settle down for a few minutes and relax and take off his jacket and shirt then get down to the job calmly and methodically and rhythmically, and reverently; but the clatter and urgency of the others outside the field on the road gathering their gear and equipment and will to press on to the next bridge or ditch or whatever target lay ahead in this dank wilderness made him drive on with his task to deafen his ears and blind his mind against what was happening and what he had volunteered to do, and above all the real reason he had volunteered to do it.

By six o'clock that evening the three children had decided to keep the body and bury it themselves.

'It's our war too, isn't it?' Kingdom appealed defiantly to the others. 'And *our* beach!'

Nancy and Frank stood transfixed and sodden, eyes glued to the body of the young airman on the grass at their feet, shivering from cold and fear and damp, unable to believe what they had just done: wade fully clothed into the waters of their secret cove and drag the enormous sodden lump of a corpse to the water's edge and lay it out like they did in the *Wizard* and the cinema.

'Why should we always do things the way adults want?' Kingdom was stuttering on as if to convince the other two who were far too immersed in their own fear and horror to take in anything he was saying.

'He came into our cove, didn't he?' Kingdom insisted anxiously, shivering and trying to cope with his own fear and horror and the awful cold in his hands and chest where he had touched the body hardest during the long strain to hold it fast through the hundred yards of waves and slippery stones and seaweed. And through the ache in his shoulders and the bruises on his hands knowing for all time the true meaning of dead weight.

'We've saved him, haven't we?'

There was rumour of confusion in the High Command as well. Montgomery and Eisenhower, of course. Or Eisenhower and Montgomery, to be more accurate. American and British. Maybe that's where the trouble lay, rivalry between the old seasoned hand forced to play second fiddle to the less-experienced master from the New World.

Of course there was no argument. The Yanks were in charge. They had the men and the power. Without them there could have been no Second Front. But it added to the uncertainty and tension. Eisenhower favoured a 'broad front' strategy, while Montgomery wanted a single all-out concentrated drive into Germany. Arnhem put paid to all that. And damp Octobers don't help.

They were not far from a place called Tilburg, not one of the names history would celebrate, Kingdom thought, but someone had to die for it or because of it. He paused, stuck his spade into the wet earth at the edge of the field and glanced at the body turned over face down on the grass. This was the difficult bit, not the digging but coming face to face, so to speak.

The others had gone ahead, but were too reluctant to meet any more war to have gone very far. There weren't any objectives around here, just more damp roads, flat, very flat fields, and the odd copse and farmhouse to break the monotony. And the occasional cheerless casualty.

Plus the garbage of course. War seemed to be all about garbage. Litter, trash, junk. Wreckage, they preferred to call it. Sounded better, more war-like. But it was garbage all the same. Even bodies were garbage; at the time, that is, in the 'heat of battle', as they say, or the damp. Until it was all over and they transmuted into heroes fit for ceremonial burials with flags and pipes and last posts and white cassocks in the Flanders wind.

But immediately after the battle, or skirmish, or *exchange* – that was the greatest sham – they were rubbish. There wasn't time to treat them as anything else. Which was why he was being so meticulous, and why the others thought him crazed. But then they didn't know about the young pilot.

He had just gone fourteen. Nancy was a year younger, Frank the same.

The body had been washed into their special cove. Shot down over one of the Atlantic convoys, the Russian convoys, and washed up a couple of nights later. The three of them had spotted it on one of their beach-combing sorties. They spent most of their spare time combing the coast in search of exciting finds, despite adult warnings of the dangers of what 'gets washed up these days'.

They scrambled down to the remote beach and found it being pounded by the waves on the incoming tide, and they waded in and hauled it ashore and hid it away in the cave and decided to keep it and give it their own ceremony. Otherwise it would be taken from them and delivered to the authorities and they would be out of the picture again.

He had dug most of the grave and Nancy had prepared the lesson and Frank had nicked the tarpaulin. The tarpaulin gave them away. Nancy had insisted they needed a shroud and he was in love with her so there was no argument and Frank was dispatched to steal one from the fishermen. Otherwise they might have got away with it. But they needed to do it their way because the war was their war too, but at their age they were only ever shushed into silence, pushed away, told they were too young, put in their place, told off, sent home, and ordered to do homework.

It was daring but they knew they could do it. The shroud let them down.

Now here again four years later, the body of a young soldier at his feet, it was up to him to arrange some shallow burial if not find a tarpaulin for it. The lesson would be all right; he could feel the words starting to come back to him with the rhythm of the digging.

But this time he wasn't rescuing him, if you can talk of rescuing the dead. He had shot him himself. As the platoon trudged along the damp Dutch road only minutes before, he had spotted the movement in the misted field and known it was a sniper and acted instinctively as he had been trained, super-tensed as he was after the last skirmish before breakfast and the screams not yet out of his head. And in a flash before anyone else so much as lifted an eye to notice, he had raised his rifle and the body pitched forward into the fence. When they reached him he was unarmed, probably trying to surrender.

He unhitched his pack and immediately went for the shovel and the sergeant said, 'Don't be bloody daft, man!' but he insisted and was admonished, 'Remorse is not the luxury of a soldier!' But he pleaded his case saying, 'It's not that, Sergeant, but it might lie there for weeks. There's no one for miles, and I did it.'

'Bollocks,' said the sergeant, 'there's nothing personal in bloody war! We *all* did it.'

'But this is different, Sergeant, if you please. It's not like in battle. It's isolated, a separate case.' The sergeant studied him, and he added, 'It's almost personal, not a real fight.'

The sergeant stared on wondering what sort of isolated case *he* had on his hands. As he heaved a deep sigh before pronouncing judgement, Kingdom raced on. 'I'll just dig him in,' he said, pointing to the still warm body appealing at their feet. 'Get him off my mind.'

But he knew full well he could never do a quick, superficial job. And maybe the sergeant knew too. But he didn't say what he would be getting off his mind, otherwise he would be a liability.

In a few moments they had left him to it, shying off, thinking he'd gone queer, and shouting to him to hurry along, but he didn't hear or care because this time he knew he was going to go through with it for all their sakes: Frank at Caen, long since unseen Nancy, the boy pilot by the sea, and now the pair of them here, somewhere on the Western Front where it was early morning and October and misty and all quiet again.

For one small moment, he would make the war a little bit of his own and direct its course in the way he wanted. Because he knew why he was here. Nothing to do with freedom and the end of tyranny, but to see things done in the same dignified manner he had tried four years before and been denied.

They left him a bike and said, 'Good luck, and make it short and shallow, mind.'

The waves rushed towards the cove as the tide which had brought the airman to them flowed, and rose and struck the beach threatening to thrash them if they didn't hurry up and take their precious find away with them otherwise it would take it back because they were dithering again and how long did they think a self-respecting tide could wait for them to make up their minds, and the waves hammered the rocks again to teach them to pay attention and get a bloody move on because there was a war on and no time to waste.

The surge was all one surge, and Kingdom knew then that whatever happened they would go through with it and bury this lost airman in the way they wanted and in the way he knew was right. And Frank neither thought nor listened but dug and dug his feet deeper into the stones to get a grip and hold and heaved on the body so that he fell back with it and it slithered from their grip.

'It's right!' Kingdom screamed above the waves whipping the rocks and stones. 'It's right!' he screamed stupidly through the spray as he got another hold and dragged and staggered. And Nancy tried to latch on to the sodden jacket and the wet material slipped through her freezing fingers and she looked at him and he saw her face standing out iced in its horror as the water slapped her hair tight around her head and her eyes and cheekbones seemed to thrust from the flesh sharp as a skull.

And she cried out to him, 'I know! I know!' but not because it was a matter of right and wrong, but because it was happening.

*   *   *

He heard a car coming, or a light truck, a jeep maybe, and he dug harder as if to force them not to take notice. Out of the corner of his eye he watched it approach and steeled himself. He wanted no discussion, no argument, no explanation. He couldn't stand being ordered to 'get the hell out of here and join your bloody unit, man!' and leave the body for the pioneers or ambulance men or whichever garbage collectors were coming up that morning. They wouldn't be out looking for much today in any case. Not much 'activity' going on.

'If we get caught we'll get hung!' Frank's words quaked and quivered as he clutched the gash down his temple from stumbling against the rocks with the weight of the waterlogged body and tried to hold on to life after the awful experience of rescuing the dead.

   'We're not doing any harm!' pleaded Kingdom.
   'Not yet.'
   'Well, then.'
   'We will if we keep him.'
   'I didn't say *keep*. I said *bury*.'
   'We'll be branded as traitors.'
   'For rescuing someone? Don't be bloody daft!'
   'Aiding and abetting the enemy.'
   'But he's dead! He can't harm anyone anymore.'

The three of them gazed down at the sodden body of the airman face down on the grass by the edge of the beach and they began to shiver and cry simultaneously as, the enormous physical struggle over, life came rushing back to them with Kingdom's last words. The real world flooded in like another thunderous wave knocking them back into this world from out of the fantasy episode they had just come through like the dream of a violent fairy tale. Now they were awake and it was evening and cold and the thing at their feet was sodden and rigid and blue and blotched and not *pretend* dead as they had seen on the cinema screen and performed themselves a hundred times, but *real* dead, stiff and wet and voiceless and staring dead, as in coffins and hearses and graveyards, and as in cats and dogs you dig in at night with a spade and a lantern at the bottom of the garden. *That* dead. That kind of dead, only more so because it was human dead and adult human to boot. And above all it was enemy dead.

It was a jeep but British. Of course. Well, it might have been Canadian because they were nearby; they had taken that other place over to the north called Bergen something or other. Funny name, with a zoom on the end of it. Funny that, French names and German he could handle: Amiens, Armentieres, Chapelle, Cambrai, and then Essen and Dortmund, Frankfurt and Dusseldorf – all a bit ahead still but he could handle them as names of war. But not Dutch; somehow they didn't fit. Not names like Neuzen or Hulst, Lokeren, Breda or Herzogenbosch. Stations on a wireless dial maybe, but not war. Daft really. He dug on.

'Should we let him dry out first?'
  'Why?'
  'Sounds better.'
  'It's all the same, isn't it?'
  'Well, I'd like to feel nice and dry before I went into a bag.'
  'Right, we'll wait.'
They steeled themselves and pulled him over the pebbles into a niche of the cave well above high water.

The cave was full of boxes and scrap planks and mattresses and bottles and cans and hordes of other articles combed from the beach that made up a children's pirate cove which they had spent years perfecting.

Kingdom and Frank rummaged around for sacking.

'He'll keep for the night. Besides, it's cool.'

'Cool!'

'All right, *freezing* then.'

They unearthed some potato bags and started to tear them open to make larger covers.

'Shall we bury him at sea?'

'No, he's an airman.'

Nancy watched and listened motionless but for her shivering.

'Besides, we'd never get a boat out in this weather, and unless we got far enough away he'd be washed back.'

'In the trees then, up the mountain?'

'The higher the better.'

'When?'

'I'll dig it tomorrow and we can do it the next morning early. It's better with a dawn burial.'

'Why?'

'It's more *right*, isn't it? Impressive.'

Nancy turned away and moaned, 'Oh, God, here I go again!' and vomited in great heaves, clutching her stomach and bending to her knees on the stones and reminding Kingdom even in the midst of the terrible tension of the scene of how they had faked dying just like that a hundred times in their games: Cowboys and Indians, Eyeties and Jerries, Cops and Gangsters, spies and crooks, everyone crumpling over gripping their guts in the same hunched-crunched attitude of Nancy.

Kingdom drove on knowing he did not have to dig so deep because he was only digging a shallow grave for the time being and yet he felt he would go on and on until he was satisfied otherwise they could just as well have left him there and thrown some brush and scrub over him or even taken off the jacket and thrown it over his head.

But he was driven on by some other command, working himself back into another time. He was no longer doing a makeshift job in the outskirts of wherever the hell on earth he was; he was back on the north-east coast with the wind lashing his freezing hands and body, aching as he drove in that spade again to loosen the earth inside the farmland fence on the cliff side, as far as possible inside to avoid driving down into solid rock and yet not too far to encroach into the field itself and risk them unearthing the body one day. It wasn't proper farmland, only a field turned over for the first time ever, because in those days every patch of green was attacked in the hope that something would grow to help with the food shortage, so the chances were a field on the side of a virtual mountain sloping down to the cliffs and exposed to wind and sea would always be a devil to cultivate and would likely be returned to its permanent fallow days once the war had gone. But in the meantime they would not stop him in the part he had to play in this bloody war.

He drove the shovel down and tore the soil from its bed and flung it aside. This time he would achieve his object and if they never ever found the body then fine, he would have done what he wanted to do years ago, and he and Nancy and Frank and that young German pilot would have been allowed to rest at last, so to speak.

He kept his eyes tight and blotted out the sounds of his platoon disappearing and he was back on the north-east coast and it was March, the same March because his body could feel all the aches and pains and colds of March, the signs of March, and the only difference was that it was on another calendar.

He bent down and held her, suddenly without thinking, clutching her in a way he would never have dared before, but now it was right and it didn't matter –

because he wanted to help her and because he needed desperately to encourage her to stay with them and help bury the German airman and because he needed to feel the throb of her through his blood and veins and body that made him shimmer and shiver at the same time and, more than any other reason in this awful business they had embarked upon, made him realise that he was doing the right thing and there were reasons beyond explanations and war and orders and commands and directives and mums warning and adults admonishing, things he sensed when he touched her and held her and smelt and felt above and beyond the vomit and the sea and the strange mixture of sand and seaweed and rock that came from the cave and the huddled body, intimations of other things that made him twitch in his groin and reminded him that it was frightening but right, like keeping the corpse, not because it was a matter of right and wrong, but because it was happening.

The faint swelled up over him as he held her, starting somewhere outside beneath the salt saturated pebbles and travelling up through his legs and thighs and guts and holding it there like cream shuddering at the top of a milk bottle or curds wobbling in a dish, and music flowing from her to him that he could neither hum nor whistle, just a singing of the whole body. And the pain of her vomiting and the horror of handling the sodden dead body did not obscure the other sensation at all.

Frank said, 'The tide will cut us off.'

The truck slowed but still he kept his head down. It almost stopped. In fact it had, hadn't it? He kept going. He was doing well. The soil was damp but it was soil. Not a trace of north-east coast rock. The engine purred on. He heard murmurs, quite pronounced in the damp air.

They wouldn't be able to see his whole body now because he was down a foot or two and the excavated soil was piling up but they would see clearly what was going on except that they just might not notice the body.

It was different the first time. He hadn't noticed he was being watched then. Not from the start of course. Now he could feel the eyes on him. At any moment he could expect a shout, or a shot. 'Go on, then!' he thought. Two can play this little game. Why don't you just get down and come over and ask. He had nothing to hide. Except a corpse of course. Not an unusual thing these days. Not like four years ago.

Frank was detailed to steal the tarpaulin.

'We must have a shroud,' insisted Nancy on the way home. 'Everybody has a shroud.'

'Won't the sacking do?' asked Frank.

'It's not waterproof.'

'What's that got to do with it? It's going underground, isn't it?'

'Because it won't be a shroud then.'

Frank shook his head but perhaps it was the pain from the wound in his temple.

'It might be difficult,' said Kingdom, trying to appease or reconcile them both.

'Then there's no point,' said Nancy, dismissive. 'Might as well hand him over to the authorities.'

'But why?'

'If it's a burial it has to be proper. So we have to have prayers, a lesson and a shroud.'

'But it won't be *proper* anyway,' pleaded Frank. 'I mean, there's no coffin or preacher or flowers or gravestone or anything.'

They were nearly home.

'I'll get the lesson and you get the spade,' she said turning to Kingdom, all pain of vomiting gone. 'But if you can't get the tarpaulin,' she said to Frank, 'the funeral's off.'

'OK.' Frank touched his temple and examined the blood clotted on his palm.

'It's not *that* bad,' said Nancy. 'But if you need me to, I'll cover up for you. They'll believe *me*.'

Despite his promise to the sergeant, he knew he was going to overdo it. He knew he was going to end up doing a proper six foot job. And if that truck hung about much longer it could be twelve. He hadn't intended to when he volunteered. The sergeant had agreed, reluctantly, sensing something not quite straight in Kingdom's plea, giving in but not completely. 'Go on, then,' he had said. 'But make it snappy. No cenotaph stuff, mind!'

Now he was into the rhythm. That first three or four minutes of deep concentration when the jeep passed had driven him on, dulling his senses, so that he stopped noticing time or effort. He went right into himself, blotting out everything. He drove himself unwittingly into a rhythm and forgot his promise to the sergeant.

And now the truck. But they didn't know he was untouchable now. They didn't know about the first jeep. They didn't know about dedication.

He thought of Montgomery and Eisenhower and wondered where they were at that moment: Ike, supremely assured with the whole map of Europe spread out before him and at his mercy, and Monty, slightly miffed, sloshing his way through Netherlands mud left to grope his way around the edges of Germany instead of the head-on Alamein push he would have preferred. And him hacking away at the dull damp Dutch earth and the silent figure beside him waiting patiently. And he marvelled that everything the three of them were doing at this moment, or the four, was interlinked, directed towards the exact same end; they were all engaged in precisely the same task, in pursuit of precisely the same objective: to *complete* the war.

This grave was an integral part of the whole design. The war would not be completed without it. Take it away, like a brick from a building, and the whole structure would collapse. It had happened once before and look what that entailed – the war had been prolonged for four years.

The following morning he left for school but dodged. He went to the allotments, strips of land on the hillside chopped up into miniature gardens so that everyone, garden or no garden, had a chance to grow food. No one gave him a second glance. Young lads were often having time off school to help with the 'War Effort' in one way or another. After half an hour he was off with the spade, dodging down the hillside gardens and out on to the coast road. There was no one around at that hour. Only the odd dog protested at his deceit.

Nancy raised a few eyebrows when she took a New Testament and Hymn Book with her to school, but she explained that 'the Bible isn't only religion. You can study it as literature too, you know.' And at school she asked her German teacher for a copy of the Lord's Prayer in German, 'and the Twenty-third Psalm if you have it.' She showed her her New Testament and Bible and Hymn Book and said she fancied doing a bit of comparison. Keenness in schoolwork was always condoned.

Frank had the difficult task. He got off school all right on account of the bad cut on his temple which now sported an ominous plaster. Then he had to go through the motions of wandering off by the beach to ease the pain and look philosophically at the sea pretending it was one way of coping with it.

He had his eyes on one of the tarpaulin sheets that covered the smaller fishing boats. Sometimes, depending on the weather and state of readiness, the fishermen slung them inside to save them the trouble of covering the boat and having to lash it in place.

But a few fishermen were around doing maintenance jobs and he might have to wait until afternoon or evening. The longer he waited the more suspicious they became, but then again pain and philosophy could take time.

Suddenly a dog barked, furiously, from a building at the far side of the field towards the Canadians, and Kingdom was right back to the morning he grabbed the garden spade and hurried off. He was shocked by the strong effect of the association. He must have heard a thousand dogs since then, but of course not so many graves.

Then, almost as if frightened off by the bark, the truck or whatever it was suddenly revved up and raced off. The dog howled it away into the distance, and then seemed to whimper on alone, disappointed that his barking had succeeded but left him with only a silent grave-digger.

He kept on digging and found himself matching the *woof, woof, woof* with the *chuff, chuff, chuff* of his spade, until the dog decided to retire and upset his rhythm and all that was left in the autumn air was the uneven *chonk, chonk, chonk* of the unaccompanied spade.

The figure on the ground waited patiently.

He worked all day on the side of the hill. It was very hard. Once he had broken through the topsoil of tough short grass ideal for sheep grazing but not tilling, the earth underneath was stony and dry and the shovel kept grating and sparking against stone. He was right by the edge of the field inside the fence where there was a slight depression. It was also on a curve of the field which gave him protection, although he knew no one would be wandering that way at this time of year.

By the middle of the afternoon he was getting some-where despite the resistance of the soil, and it would have been more than deep enough for a temporary grave. Being at the edge too and in the slight hol-low it was likely to be out of reach of any plough. And when the war ended and the field reverted to fallow it would never be noticed. That was the only thought that jarred that day: that this man's grave would be forever unmarked, and his family would never know.

Nancy spent the day writing out a simple service and practising some German. She would use only selected sentences or phrases and have them written down so there would be no problem. She just felt that something had to be said in the man's own language even if far from perfect, like 'thy Kingdom come' and 'goodness and mercy' and 'The Lord's my shepherd' of course. That was always a good one for funerals. Essential in fact. Like a shroud.

Frank had a futile day pretending he was convalesc-ing and only incidentally interested in tarpaulins. By mid morning he was feeling superconscious and had contemplated the ocean long enough for him to write a treatise on philosophy.

He broke for lunch which meant he wandered off and walked along the south shore and killed time by doing some honest beach-combing. But he was terri-fied he might find another body, although he was not sure if his fear was to do with being all on his own this time or of having to locate another tarpau-lin.

He wandered back in the afternoon and again tried hard to appear nonchalant.

When he paused at long last but only for a few moments he noticed that the mist had lifted slightly over in the direction of the Canadians, the farm buildings and the dog. Visibility was still very bad this morning, or autumn, but he could make out three small stacks of hay covered in black tarpaulin lashed to the ground.

Well, now, he thought, relaxing for the first time, there's a nice bit of baksheesh. It was all coming together, wasn't it? And a voice said, 'Everybody has a shroud.'

He was finished by sunset.

Nancy had arrived at five o'clock and read him her suggested sermon and text. It sounded fine, in fact very impressive. Probably very exact too, as befits someone pernickety about shrouds.

Frank was late. And nervous when he arrived. He had had to wait until nearly dark before he could risk doing the deed and he was afraid that when they noticed it had gone the following morning he would be the only suspect because he had hung about the beach all day and there was a limit to how long fishermen would commiserate with pain and meditation.

They had to meet before daybreak and it was up to each to find an excuse for leaving home in the middle of the night.

Some of the phrases kept coming back to him now, jogged out of his memory by the action of swinging and digging and the effect of the rawness of the air. It was very similar, in fact he could feel the presence of the others as the words came back to him:

for man is not made by bread alone
we are not born of flesh and blood
we wrestle against spiritual wickedness in high places

– which he didn't understand but thought had something to do with adults not allowing children to play their full part in the war:

> *in the full and certain belief of the Resurrection*
> *Thy kingdom come*

– which he had asked for because it had such a ring of authority and gave him his nickname, and

> *der Herr ist mein Hirte*
> *unser Vater im Himmel*
> *Gutes und Barmherzigkeit*

and

> *ich werde bleiben im Hause des Herrn immerdar*

Gosh, it was all coming back.

They were there before dawn and he and Frank dragged the body all the way up the hillside frightened that it would literally disintegrate in their hands and slither away back down the hill in soggy pieces.

But they made it and wrapped it tenderly in Frank's tarpaulin and manoeuvred it to the grave.

At the moment they dumped it on to the black tarpaulin it transmuted into a shroud and Nancy started her readings. It took some time for them to get the body suitably wrapped and she went through all her material before they got ready to lower it into the grave. But she said it didn't matter, the first run was like a dress rehearsal and she was glad of the time because she hadn't had much practice and it gave her the chance to get her tongue around the difficult words.

Then they began to lower the body and she started up again:

> *der Herr ist mein Hirte*
> *for we wrestle not against flesh and blood*
> *the meek shall inherit the earth*
> *Gutes und Barmherzigkeit*
> *goodness and mercy*

and

> *im Hause des Herrn immerdar*

When he finished digging he thought it had taken a lot less time than the first, but he was older and the soil here was much easier and apart from the truck there was no tension and he was not confronting death for the first time.

And he reflected that war was not the beautifully organised conflicts of the *Adventure* and the *Wizard*, but a shambles like the tool shed on the allotment and the drawers in his room which he had been consistently told to tidy up before the Germans decided there were more important things for growing boys to be getting on with. Amazing how the war had got into everything.

He wiped his hands on the wet grass and dried them on his trousers.

But they weren't allowed to finish. A warden on his vigil along the hill road overlooking the coastline had spotted them through his binoculars and raised the alarm. It was his job to keep watch along a five mile stretch of the coast, to keep his eyes out for anything suspicious, anything washed in or landed, any barrels or stray mines or other unusual objects. Bodies, maybe, too but that was seldom though not unheard of. The odd suicide, and once or twice the washed-up remains from a downed aircraft or stricken ship. He did his first tour at daybreak and his last at sunset. They should have remembered.

This morning he was on special lookout: for a boy leaving the beach yesterday evening shrouded in mystery and a stolen tarpaulin.

Through his powerful binoculars he still could not identify what they were doing down there on the edge of the field by the cliff top, because they were working below the dip and the sun was rising into his lenses; but they seemed to be burying something, something washed up no doubt. Silly buggers, could be something bloody dangerous. Although they were in silhouette they were kids sure enough but this was war and no one was allowed to do anything even slightly out of the ordinary. Three youngsters on a hilltop overlooking a dangerous section of north-east coast, digging desperately at dawn by the edge of a field and intent on burying some dark package could not be passed over. He made for the farm.

The posse of eight armed men rounded the bend and caught them in full view, the body already in the shallow grave they must have broken their arms and backs digging, Kingdom and Frank waiting patiently with their heads hung in the freezing wind, and Nancy with her page spread out struggling bravely through her quotations.

He looked towards the buildings and stacks still haloed in mist.

No, he thought, surveying his work and his blistered hands, the patient body and the hovering mist, war was not all glamorous and staged and choreographed in open green fields.

He walked across the field towards the stacks and unhitched the tarpaulin. He started to fold it but thought it a waste of time and he set off dragging it behind him, picking up on the thought about war not being glamorous but about squelching around on soggy strips of land no one would have planted on anyway, and searching for makeshift shrouds on wet beaches and misted farms.

The dog kept stumm.

The powers were even more shocked. It became a scandal

rather than an escapade. Minors or not, the charge was serious, because this was wartime and they had been 'handling' the enemy. Not to mention the stolen tarpaulin. The interrogations went on and involved parents, teachers, vicars, army, and sundry darker men with even more power stamped over them imported from distant parts to pronounce darker judgements. They were taken into care, branded as 'the deadly three', and despised because they had shown respect to and harboured a Hun. There was something morbid in what they had done. There was also something disloyal. It was an unholy combination.

Worst of all they were separated. They called it evacuation. Never saw each other again. But he heard that Frank had died at Caen and that Nancy's parents, in shame, had moved from the area.

Now the dog barked again and he paused to scan the field and road but nothing was coming so he spread out the tarpaulin and rolled the body on to it, and then rolled them up together thinking that Ike and Monty depended upon him, and Nancy and Frank too.

The dog barked again and he twisted to look in the direction of the stacks and buildings and thought he detected movement through the damp mist that was hovering and weaving patterns, and he imagined a posse of eight armed men charging out from behind the stacks. In fact the movement was the sun striving to push aside the mist. He was grateful for that. He turned the body so that it was near enough facing east.

He dropped down into the hole and stamped the ground firmly under his feet and pulled the body in. It was the only way. As he settled it in position, Nancy's voice came back to him:

Gutes und Barmherzigkeit
werden mir folgen mein Leben lang

goodness and mercy shall follow me
through all the days of my life

When he raised himself erect again his feet astride the body, he could just see over the mound of earth that lay between him and the far fence. He pulled himself up to kneel on the edge and leaned forward to his rifle and spade propped on the mound, and in his crouched position lifted the spade to scoop in some earth as if raising a rifle.

The dog barked again and he looked up across the field in time to see the figure drop on its knees and the puff of smoke, and he toppled back with his spade lifted in the air as if brandishing his rifle.

SONG LINE

Aachen, October 1944

Six

We're gonna hang out the washing
on the Siegfried Line.
Have you any dirty washing, Mother dear?
We're gonna hang out the washing
on the Siegfried Line,
'Cos the washing day is here.

Preparing his socks for hanging on the Siegfried Line, Magna Carter said, 'I have to do it, lads. I promised them back home I would. I can't let them down.'

'How will they know you've done it, Magna?'

'I got some photographer chappie coming up from Paris.'

'Could take him weeks.'

'Listen, there's a lot of folks back there waiting to see that song in the flesh. Not just Vera *singing* it. *Photographs* of it.'

When Magna was evacuated from Sheffield in the winter of '39, he landed up in a tiny village down in Devon, somewhere in the no man's land between Tipton St Michael and Ottery St George. No more than a pub and a shop and a few farmers' cottages. And Mad Manor.

'But everyone was mad there, not just up at the manor.'

It took him a long time to get used to the cold air and the strong light because Magna had been brought up inside the pall of Sheffield that enclosed the city like a grip of steel. 'Only it wasn't steel. It was smoke. You could climb up in the hills just outside and see it lying there under this great steel tarpaulin.'

Only, they never got up there much and when they did it was only for a short time and then they had to go on down again and slip back under the blanket. 'We lived under it all the time. Never used to see light, I mean real light, with nothing between you and it, until I reached this place.'

Magna wandered about staring at the sky and wondering where the tarpaulin was and shivering because he didn't have his great blanket to keep him warm and the villagers used to think he was a bit ga-ga. 'But not ga-ga like they was. I was just displaced, you know, out of my depths, trying to get the hang of this fresh place and the fact that other people had been living this clean life all the years I'd been living under my steel shroud.'

It took him months to get used to the light that smarted his eyes and the funny things that kept coming in through his mouth and tingling his throat. 'Fresh air and sunlight isn't everyone's birthright, you know.'

But they looked after him because they knew he must be homesick. 'Only I never figured out how they knew what homesick meant because, sure as hell, they'd never been out of that place for a day in their lives.' They must have been protecting him because they thought him out of his mind like themselves. And they were that way because they kept sending their sons and dads and husbands and brothers to war 'and getting them brown paper envelopes telling them they weren't coming back'. Turned them barmy, 'but not so barmy as them up at Mad Manor.'

Whether the weather may be wet or fine,
We'll just rub along without a care.
We're gonna hang out the washing
on the Siegfried Line
If the Siegfried line's still there!

After the Normandy landings in June 1944 the Allied forces put over two million men on the mainland of Europe and during the next four months waged the so-called 'second battle of France'.

By September they had driven the German armies back to behind their long line of fortifications stretching from Basel in the south to Düsseldorf in the north which marked Germany's pre-war frontier. This massive line of defence was known as the West Wall, and more familiarly as the Siegfried Line. To get there it cost the Allies 40,000 dead, 165,000 wounded and 20,000 missing. It cost the Germans half a million.

'Tampering' with the Siegfried Line was like 'tampering' with the Rhine. There was more to it than the military achievement. They were defence lines of another kind. They *meant* Germany.

Magna got to know the village by just wandering around. There wasn't far to go and there wasn't a lot to see, but he was in awe of all the light and the air, and got to know the people and they treated him as one of the family despite their reputation for being cut off and living in their own little time warp and desert island. 'They had time for me,' said Magna, 'but more like people take kindly to a stray animal than a strange human being.' But it didn't matter to him. He got treated well, 'I wasn't a stranger for long, but *they* was strange for ever.'

They treated him well in his new home too, no more than a tight farmer's cottage, but he had his own room which is more than he could have dreamed of in

Sheffield. 'It was only a bit of a box but enough for me and my own and you wondered how they could spare it but they did.' They had no children of their own, so they spent extra time on him because they had to learn how to cope with one.

'I was like their first-born, see, and they took a pride in me because of that and were grateful they didn't have to go through all the pains of birth and teething and measles and nappies. They got off easy 'cos I came potty trained.'

So Magna found himself mollycoddled by two sets of new parents: his foster ones in the cottage and the whole village family.

'The place was full of crazed people all gathering around doors, listening to the news on the wireless, desperately waiting for letters, clinging to hopes and beliefs, and singing wartime songs, like *Run, Rabbit* and *White Cliffs* and *Wing and a Prayer* and the *Siegfried Line washing* one. Proper mad house. Like they was eating some kind of herb.'

'Any old bit of wall or tank will do, Magna! They'd never tell the difference?'

'Couldn't do that to them! Not right. Besides, they're not so ga-ga. They'd spot lies like that.'

The popular song *'We're gonna hang out the washing on the Siegfried Line'* swept the Home Front as early as the optimistic days of 1939 when hopes were high it would all be over by Christmas. But the promise faded rapidly after Dunkirk and the Blitz when the war reached out to places far beyond the border of Germany and France where the Siegfried Line stood. Another jolly tune to keep the peckers up faded during the dark years of the early 1940s when nothing seemed capable of halting the German military machine and 'victory' was the name one dared not speak.

The nation had to wait until 1944 before Churchill could proclaim that 'the tide of war' had turned and 'the mists had cleared from the horizon' and the end was in sight. The optimistic songs could be dug out from the music chest and sung again with confidence.

> *Mother dear I'm writing you*
> *From somewhere in France*
> *Hoping this finds you well.*
> *Sergeant says I'm doing fine:*
> *'A soldier and a half'.*
> *Here's the song that we'll all sing,*
> *It'll make you laugh.*

For the first time since the German invasion of Austria in March 1938, Siegfried was back where he belonged, behind his own garden wall. Breaching the Siegfried Line, like crossing the Rhine, had profound symbolic meaning. The very names rang of Germany. Conquer them and victory would be assured:

> *We're gonna hang out the washing*
> *on the Siegfried Line . . .*

Magna told his mates that the French photographer chappie would take the pictures of him and his socks as soon as he got there.

'But it's one helluva long line, Magna! How will he know where to look?'

'He'll know. People know things like that – instinctively.'

'You must be out of your mind.'

'I was once.'

Magna's unit was at least 100 miles north of the nearest point of contact with the Siegfried Line fortifications, somewhere in the region of Koblenz. But Monty wasn't going that way and so neither was Magna. If he had any hopes of seeing the Siegfried Line he would have to drop out and hitch a lift to the south. Then if he survived he would have to meet up with Bradley's Americans who would be pretty bushed by then and probably not particularly friendly to a wandering, wayward limey from somewhere in the far north. His presence might take a bit of explaining to a tired group on a short fuse.

'If the sergeant don't catch you, Magna, the Yanks will.'

'They're OK. They'll understand.'

'Magna, mate, do you really think they'll listen to a cock and bull story about hanging out washing on a line from an unknown limey with an accent smelling like strong scrumpy moseying around waiting for an unknown frog photo bloke to turn up and take snaps of your bleeding socks! Do us a favour, will you!'

'Well,' said Magna, reflectively, 'we'll see.'

The war could have been on another planet let alone a million miles away but its effect on the village between Michael and George was shattering.

When Magna arrived a couple of their men had already gone missing out of a population of one thousand and twenty-five and it was still only Christmas 1939. And there was another fifteen to go, three a year.

'Couldn't think how they found all them able-bodied men in such a small place. The war was like some plague or pest that crept in from outside and knocked off all the young males. They had that stunned look as if they would never do anything again except prop up fences and doors. Only contact with the outside world was the postman who kept on bringing all them brown envelopes.

'But they never stopped singing that song.'

Everybody's mucking in
And doing their job,
Wearing the great big smile.
Everybody's got to keep
Their spirits up today.
If you want to keep in swing
Here's the song to sing.

'Anyway, how will you know if your photographer chappie's coming?'

'I won't. But I do.'

'Irish.'

'No, French actually.'

'Maybe he's not alive either.'

'Well, more chance he is than us.'

'And if he don't turn up before we move on, then what?'

'I'll have to leave them, won't I?'

'Leave your bleeding socks on the line!'

'Got any other ideas?'

'But if the wind don't get them, somebody'll nick em.'

'Got to take that chance.'

'And if he does come and takes a picture, what's he going to do with it?'

'Send it to my foster-mum.'

'Got her address, has he?'

'Gave it him the night we met in Caen.'

'Thought you said Paris.'

'I met him at Caen but he comes from Paris.'

'Bloody months ago. Could be anywhere.'

'Well, like I said, you got to take the chance.'

'Anyway, how will he know they're yours?'

'Gotta take that chance too.'

'And how will your foster-mum know they're yours?'

'Oh, she'll know. She knitted them. Tell them a mile off.'

*We're gonna hang out the washing
on the Siegfried Line.
Have you any dirty washing, Mother dear?*

Outside the village proper stood a large house like a
mediaeval manor. It was quite a way off and built on
a small hill in its own grounds surrounded by a high
wall and dense woodland firs, and the only entrance
was past a run-down lodge guarded by an enormous
senile St Bernard which was always sound asleep by
the main gate that had rusted and could no longer be
closed.

Magna got the job delivering the mail and the daily
papers to Mad Manor as it was known because no one
else wanted to make the trek after the regular lad was
called up. Each time he got to within a few hundred
yards of the gate he could hear the music of the
Siegfried Line coming from a gramophone somewhere
inside.

'Turned out to be some lord's place. He'd got himself
killed at the Somme so the family gave it to the British
Legion to make a home for all the men maimed in the
bloke's regiment, he being the CO, see.

'I used to deliver the mail and papers every morning
and sometimes I'd get in at the back door and they'd
give me a cup of tea and a sandwich with homemade
butter and an extra egg, 'cos they had their own stuff and
weren't so strict on the old rations. It was like having your
own private farm and no one ever coming to see you on
account of what you kept there.'

'What was that, then?'

'I'm coming to that. It was a fair walk from the village,
see, so I needed a bit of sustenance when I arrived and I
got to hanging about in the kitchens and doing odd jobs
for them 'cos they didn't have any able-bodied people left
and were mostly older women. Took some time before

they allowed me in, mind, 'cos it was all so secretive and hushed when I first started. Course, no one ever said, least of all the family I was with, 'cos all they wanted was for me to get a couple of extra bob on the papers to supplement the pittance they got to keep me and the odd bit of bacon or butter from Mad Manor.

'Soon's you got within earsight you heard the music. Went on all the time. Same old song:

> *We're gonna hang out the washing*
> *on the Siegfried Line,*
> *'Cos the washing day is here.'*

Behind the Siegfried Line the battered German Army was gathering itself for what it knew would be the Allies' final push into the heartland of the Third Reich, and their homeland. But both Bradley with the US Twelfth in the south and Montgomery with the British Second in the north had different ideas about where that final thrust should be.

Operation Market Garden was their attempt to seize key bridges across Dutch and German rivers and outflank the Siegfried Line – *Garden* the ground phase and *Market* the airborne. The US took their bridges at Maas and Waal, but the British didn't at Arnhem, and the link-up could not be made.

Then, under Model and von Rundstedt, the German forces performed the amazing feat of getting back behind the Siegfried defences and recovering enough to mount a massive defence along their West Wall.

Magna had a double problem: how to get permission to go and how to cover the hundred miles between his unit and Bradley's.

When Magna finally got to see into Mad Manor proper after a year of doing odd jobs, 'I nearly died! There wasn't no more than bits of people they kept there, like in a spare box for a Meccano set.

'They were like specimens, museum pieces. But I learned they were not natural freaks, but soldiers who'd been at the Somme in 1916. When they brought them back they couldn't look after them in an ordinary hospital and nor could their families, see, because their needs was so special, so they put them in this *extra*-special home. Most of them couldn't move and most of them couldn't even talk, and most of them could do a lot less than that.'

Magna got to know the inmates and staff and learned 'a bit about war and what it does to people', just by watching them and figuring it out for himself, 'cos 'they never uttered a dickie bird about it, their war or our one.' He worked there regularly, 'otherwise these old girls would have been on their own. Couldn't have that. Staff went around like zombies too. Maybe had to to do the job. And it got that after a year or two I couldn't tell the difference between all them up there and all them down in the village. Maybe I became one of them myself. But I tell you, I never wanted to come here and risk all that, believe me.'

'Why did you come then?'

'Fear. Stark bloody fear they'd shoot me. And the *Siegfried Line* of course.'

During the autumn and winter of '44 the Allies battered away and the Germans struck back at the Battle of the Bulge – *Operation Wacht am Rhein*. The Ardennes offensive halted the Allied advance but at tremendous cost to the Germans, and the cutting edge of their army had gone. They had succeeded in blocking the Allied left flank to the north but only to weaken their own left flank to the south, and the Yanks were through. Wherever that was, Magna was going there.

'So I got this photograph chappie coming up from Montmartre with his big studio camera. Met him in Caen and caught up with him in Paris weeks after the liberation. He was still pissed. He was a nice bloke but didn't speak much English but I told him about my mission and he said he understood and I could count on him and he'd promise to come and do it for me – or for the folks back home, that is. I told him I was sorry I couldn't give him an exact date or rendezvous but that didn't seem to worry him because he could work these things out himself and anyway he had a good calendar so I wasn't to worry my tiny tête, just to be sure and get there. Nice sort of chap. Anyway, you blokes just go on ahead. I'll see what I can work out and I'll catch you up.'

'What you really mean is you'll get yourself down there and wait for him?'

'I didn't say that.'

'How long?'

'Oh, I dunno.'

'How will you get there – hitch a lift?'

'I'll get there.'

'They'll get you for desertion.'

'We'll see.'

Have you any dirty washing, Mother dear?

When the Germans took back the Rhineland in 1936, they built their West Wall, or Siegfried Stellung, to make sure no more foreigners ever got through again: thousands of concrete bunkers and pill-boxes and observation posts and, sticking up out of the earth to stop tanks, rows of concrete pyramids like dragons' teeth, lower at the front and rising to about six feet; then huge tiers of steel beams that swung in and out like garden gates made of steel girders, and each one guarded by pill-boxes.

Hitler thought he would need the line at the beginning of the war but he was so successful he never did. He advanced so quickly and got away with so much it was soon miles behind him, and over the years it became neglected and overgrown and a bit out of date when the Yanks arrived in the autumn of 1944. The old defences were not up to much anymore but at least they delayed the Allies.

But by then the real effect and power of the Siegfried Line was its symbolism. Siegfried meant Germany. The Rhineland meant Germany. The Rhine meant Germany and Siegfried meant the Rhine and the Rhine meant Siegfried and Germany meant both and so on. Put them altogether and you have something to shout and fight about.

Both sides knew that when the Siegfried Line went it would be all over.

'Said he'd meet me at Aix. Aachen to you. Charlemagne's place.'

'But it's a million to one chance, Carter.'

'Better odds than most of us get out here.'

'Anyway, what's the bleeding point!'

'Like I said, faith. Proof. Honour the old song.'

'The Siegfried Line one?'

'Course. They don't just write songs for nothing, you know. They have a purpose, a meaning. Have to, otherwise people wouldn't give them the time of day.'

'Three minutes?'

'Even three minutes.' Magna tried a few bars:

> *Whether the weather may be wet or fine,*
> *We'll just rub along without a care.*

'You see', he went on, 'it won't be over for them down there until they see the Siegfried Line's been taken down. You could offer them the Rhine or Berlin, or Rommel or the Brandenburg Gate. Wouldn't mean a thing. But

Siegfried means everything. And if you get as far as hanging washing on someone's back line then the door's open and you're in. The journey's over. And their men can come home.'

> *Whether the weather may be wet or fine,*
> *We'll just rub along without a care.*

When it got close to his time to be called up the whole village kept at it, 'Magna, you get yourself to that old Siegfried Line now and send us back a snap of your washing on it, won't you?'

At first he thought it a great lark. But they kept it up, down in the village and up at the manor. The idea, like the music, permeated their lives. The Siegfried Line had become their life-line.

He had been through four years with them and seen all their brown envelopes and Mad Manor, and he knew it was no lark. They meant it. They believed there *was* a line.

> *We're gonna hang out the washing*
> *on the Siegfried Line*
> *If the Siegfried Line's still there!*

Shortly after six in the morning, an empty truck drew up beside the lone figure standing by the roadside holding his bag in the air. Deftly and silently, Magna swung up under the empty tarpaulin behind the driver's cab and the truck revved off. Someone moved among the bank of huddled soldiers trying to ignore the coming day.

'Wha'ss up?'

'Magna.'

'Wha'ss up?'

'Gone.'

'Whoo wiff?'

'Dunno.'
'One of ours?'
'Didn't see no markings.'
'Christ, it's bloody cold.'

What they didn't know in the village was that, as the days got nearer and nearer the time for him to be called up, Magna was getting closer and closer to making his breakaway because there was no way he was going to go off and fight and come back as a brown envelope or a permanent b&b at Mad Manor.

He was determined to desert, evaporate, and he didn't have much doubt about where he would evaporate to. And he thought the whole community would be behind him, especially when they realised that he too might soon become a brown envelope.

But even after four years he had miscalculated. They needed their Siegfried Line more. It was far more important that he go and send back the proof that it was all over even if he took the risk of not coming back at all.

They had been singing that song since Florrie Forde sang it to them in 1939. It was the village theme, their own little national anthem. And they wouldn't give it up until someone proved Fritz was back in his own yard and peace was back in theirs.

'I had it all worked out. I was going to do my bunk right there at Mad Manor. Nobody would think anyone in his right mind would want to stay there. And nobody would let on 'cos they needed me. I could have done the disappearing act and no one'd ever have known or cared.

'But no. "Go on, Magna!" they shouted. "Go on! Get over there and sent us a picture. Then we'll believe it. Then we'll know it's forever and ever. No more brown envelopes. No more Mad Manors."'

Magna was cornered.

* * *

Magna was rattled along rutted roads for four hours with only two stops while the driver got out, unhitched cans from underneath the vehicle and poured strong smelling petrol into the tank. They drove through water that slushed and swished up over the wheels and often threatened to stop the truck completely as if they were negotiating streams and shallow river-beds. Whenever possible, during lulls between rev-vings and lurchings, Magna dozed amid piles of sacks and empty crates.

He had little idea of the geography and wasn't at all dismayed by the thought. He had no idea how anyone had any idea of geography in Europe anymore. All he had seen since landing in Normandy on D-Day plus Three was destruction, not the countryside so much as the dev-astated machinery of war that littered it. Maps became more and more useless by the hour as the debris of battle obliterated and altered and confused every contour and turn of landscape. It was as if the Allied armies were advancing by instinct, roughly, very roughly, towards the east. Had they given him a map and asked him to find his way to the nearest units of the American army and the Siegfried Line fortifications he wouldn't have known which way to read it and relate it.

He had learned the basic rules of map reading, but none of that training would have made a blind bit of difference now. Getting to the Siegfried Line would not be a matter of fine map reading or geographical know-how. It could only be by chance. And chance was a fine thing.

'And the more *they* believed it, the more *I* had to too. And of course there *is* a line, isn't there? Got to be. And it's got to be possible to hang your socks on it, and take a picture and send it back to them. Because all these things are true anyway and not just songs for laughs. It's every bit as real as Mad Manor and brown envelopes.

'That's what I told my photographer friend. And that's why I know he'll be there.

'Most of us have a reason. There's not many of us here by chance or choice after Normandy.'

As he bumped and rattled along, Magna thought of the chance that had put him there in the first place since the day they had thrust him on a train with a label and a gas mask and a thousand other bewildered children: Sheffield, evacuation, Devon, Tipton, Mad Manor, brown envelopes, a song, a Siegfried Line, a French photographer – all chance.

When he got up that morning he had no idea of where he was going except the Siegfried Line. The truck just happened. Had he tried to work out any date or place or dead reckoning or grid reference, it would have been a shambles. Europe was a shambles. The only way to deal with a shambles was to shamble along in it, play it at its own game.

When at last the truck lunged to a halt, Magna clambered down and saw more ruins and spotted the gun emplacement by the pill-box nestling between rows of dulled grey concrete dragon teeth and mangled steel with its barrels askew, thrusting through piles of concrete rubble and rusted steel and a few GIs smoking, and he knew he had found the spot.

He walked away from the truck without so much as a backward glance to the driver who never got out, and as he advanced towards the crippled gun barrels that would carry his socks he heard the truck rev up and disappear from his life in exactly the way it had entered, and for the same reason all the rest of the things had happened to him in this war: no reason.

'Which part of the actual line you looking for, bud?'

asked the concerned GI sergeant. 'Wouldn't want you coming all this way and choosing the wrong heap of shit, would we?'

'Well, the first part I come across will do, thank you very much.'

The sergeant looked around at the heap of twisted German armour that might have been a shelter once, then again might have been a buried tank, then again might have been any heap anywhere in this war.

'You sure this'll do ya?'

'Oh, sure, fine by me, Sergeant. Just as long as it's the genuine article.'

The sergeant looked the mountain of destruction up and down. 'Well, I guess it was genuine once,' he conceded. 'Help yourself.'

'Thank you, Sergeant.'

Magna looked about him and began wandering around to view and assess the chosen pile as if to establish where he would hang his socks when the French photographer got there from Paris. The sergeant sucked his cheeks as he turned to his crew lounging around their jeep.

'You got all his details, Rimsky?'

'I got them, Sarge.'

'Well, this war sure sends up all sorts of problems for the common man,' said the sergeant. 'And I guess he's the one we're fighting it for.' He shrugged again.

'Only question is who's this guy got something in common *with*?' asked someone.

'Well, he sure belongs somewhere. Papers are OK. Just a bit far from home I'd say. Right, Rimsky?'

'Right on, Sarge.'

'Want maybe we should take him in for checking, Sarge?' asked another.

'Naw. He's got something to work out. Best leave him be.'

And with that he clambered back into the jeep and

the others stubbed out their cigarettes and climbed in and the driver switched on and eased away and they all stared back silently at the lone figure wandering around the heap of metal and rubble searching for a place for his socks and an angle for the French cameraman to film them from.

'You got his details, there, Rimsky?' the sergeant asked as they drove off.

'Right here, Sarge.'

'What'd he say his name was?'

'Carter, Sarge. Magna Carter.'

The sergeant sucked his cheeks again and settled back. 'Well', he said, 'guess that figures.'

'You ever hear tell of old Magna?'

'Nope.'

'Maybe he just went on home thinking he'd done his bit.'

'Probably farming somewhere.'

'Some manor in Silesia, maybe?'

'Somewhere like that.'

SHROPSHIRE LAD

The Ardennes, 22nd December 1944

Seven

Watching the line of prisoners file past him into the copse, Reevers thought he'd been here before, and he had, last year in fact, and it wasn't Germany but Shropshire where he had been evacuated from the smoke of Northumberland to help out on the land. And one thing he was observing now was that, like the German prisoners sent to work in the fields back home, this lot were not much older than himself, and when they had walked through the cold potato fields with him, as they now walked through the icy ditch to the copse where he would guard them, they looked like a ragged line of pals from his school – 'only more fair'.

Major Archie Bennett waited until they had shuffled into position huddled up in drooping greatcoats and items of ill-fitting tattered clothing then ordered, 'Right Reevers, tell this shower in their own lingo to sit down and wrap up and if they dare make a move you'll let them have one where it hurts.'

'Sir!'

Reevers cleared his throat and lifted his rifle, but before he could utter so much as an *achtung*, the major added, 'I'll be with CO Yanks for about an hour, Reevers, but the GIs will relieve you a.s.a.p. Carry on.'

'Sir!'

Completely ignoring the dubious menace of Reevers'

rifle, the ragged German group immediately squatted down on the crisp snow, and began chatting among themselves like schoolboys when the master has left the room. They pulled out cigarettes and huddled around each other to share matches and made so much noise they couldn't possibly hear Reevers' feeble order to separate, 'Wollen sie bitte . . . einen Augenblick warten' – Hold on a minute, if you don't mind.

Reevers had so welcomed the fresh air and open vistas of Shropshire that he stopped missing home less than a month after he was evacuated in the autumn of 1939 when he was thirteen. One sodden Thursday in November they had shipped him down from Ashington and shuffled him on to the station at Newcastle with his brown cardboard case in his hand and gas mask and label around his neck and thrust him into the middle of crowds of bewildered children of all ages.

He had cried when he said goodbye to his mum and dad and three sisters in their miner's terraced cottage, and cried when the bus drove them through Ashington streets black with coal smoke and dark rain. And he had felt ashamed because he was one of the bigger boys and he knew he ought to be 'setting an example', but he had never been away from home before, except to Newcastle sometimes when his uncle took him to see United because his dad was only interested in fishing when he was not down the pit, it being 'crowded enough down there and tight enough up here in this pokey little hovel, what do I need to go standing in the rain with thirty thousand others for?'

Yet within a month Reevers was another person. He had discovered space and colour and air and light. At home in Ashington, everything was cramped – the house, the street, the school. And everything was dark – the house, the street, the school. You needed artificial light, gas, lamps or candles, even in summer. And all colours were shades of black, variations on a theme of coal. 'Air' was the thick, dense smoggy stuff you cut your way through to school and the thick, dense smoggy stuff that was supposed to shield you from the glare of the sun, except that it never came through, and from the cold of the pure air, except that it rarely drifted down.

'When did you last see a white Christmas, Reevers?' asked Major Archie Bennett on the way down to Bastogne on a liaison mission to the Americans. There were lots of these quick trips that autumn, short, sharp dashes between the British and Canadian forces to the north holding the Antwerp-Liege line and the American forces in the Ardennes.

'I think there was one in Ashington once, sir,' said Reevers, peering through the snow-charged wipers.

'Ashington?'

'In Northumberland, sir.'

'Ah, well, there would be up there, wouldn't there?' observed Major Bennett authoritatively.

'Well, I only remember one, sir,' said Reevers, resolutely clutching his steering wheel. 'Even so I could be mistaken. I was pretty young then.'

He would remember *this* one. The Allies knew Hitler would make at least one big stand before they reached the frontier into Germany. Except that what was happening in the Ardennes that December was more than a big stand; it was a full-scale offensive. They hadn't bargained for that, and then.

Since Normandy, the Allies hadn't had it all their own way, but the tide was in their favour. Yet sooner or later the Germans would have to turn and take their chance to break the relentless if slow advance of the Allies. The Americans had furnished the full front of the drive. From October to December they had been hammering

away all along the German fortified zone of the Siegfried
Line while the weather steadily deteriorated until snow
was everywhere; but still the breakthrough hadn't come.
Then the first part of December brought a lull. At last
both battle-weary and weather-worn sides ground to a
halt, as if holding up their arms and saying, 'Hold it, hang
on a minute, let's have a breather. Don't know about you,
but this war's killing me.'

Then von Runstedt struck. Rallying his battered troops
he launched a sudden titanic retaliation intended to break
the hesitating Yanks and drive on through the British and
Canadians to the north and up to Antwerp. It nearly
worked. And when Major Archie Bennett climbed into
his light truck beside Driver Reevers for his quick liaison
dash south it was in fact still working.

'White or wet', he observed as the dreary miles rumbled on, 'it's one helluva way to spend Christmas!'

In the fields of Weaveney Reevers learned about colour
and perspective. Colour was what made all plants and
trees different; perspective was seeing a horizon.

Even when he got the chance to go back home for a
week he never took it. Not that he didn't want to see his
mum and dad and sisters again but because he knew he
could never tell them what he was going through. How
do you explain colour to the blind or horizons to the
short sighted? And he didn't want to tell them because
he knew they would never be able to have the chance he
was having. That was war for you.

He was leading another kind of life and wanted
nothing to disturb it. He worked whenever he could
in the fields of the farm he was billeted on. He worked
with crops and animals, sowing and reaping wheat and
barley, planting and gathering potatoes, walking to the
horizon with the collies to herd cattle and count sheep
and rounding them up to bring them home. As long as

he was outside Reevers was content; even in the worst of weather he preferred it out there, like a man who had spent his life in prison and daren't go inside again for fear he would be trapped.

But school was OK. The rooms were light and the windows large and the 'blackboard' green and the walls golden. He was at ease and learning. You could learn in a place like this. The darkness of coal and war were very far away.

The Allied forces had been sleeping, or nodding off, when von Rundstedt turned in December '44. Or at best they were unsuspecting. It never entered their minds that he had the stomach or the organisation let alone the power and cheek to make a fight of it there and then. It was a complete tactical surprise as the Panzer Armies shattered two US Divisions, causing Patton to hold off his offensive in the south and shift it north to help out, and Monty to swing his reserves south to do the same.

Von Runstedt mustered twenty-four German divisions, ten of them armoured, *and* the morale. And the Allied Air Force was nowhere because the weather had closed in. Von Runstedt noticed weather.

'We're not fighting fools, you know,' observed the sharp Major Bennett.

'No, sir,' agreed the tactful Driver Reevers, peering through the freezing fog.

'Manteuffel's Panzers, see. That's what's done it.'

'Yes, sir.'

'And Brandenburger's, of course.'

'Yes, sir.'

'They're the ones who've done the damage. Bloody fine troops, they are. *And* bloody fine officers!'

Reevers broadened his argument, 'Are they the ones we're expecting our way, sir?'

'No. It's Dietrich's Sixth who'll be calling on us.'

The wipers whirred excitedly.

'Dietrich, sir?' asked Reevers.

'Hmm.'

Reevers changed down decisively. 'Any relation, sir?'

He took an icy bend in bottom and revved out of it in second while Major Bennett pondered the question.

'D'you know, Reevers, I don't really *know* that one,' he said, puzzled and reflective, as if he had not been paying attention at Sandhurst. 'Must have a word with him when he comes.'

At school Reevers always sat by a window and looked out over the fields.

After a year he began to learn German, but more because of the classroom and the numbers. There were only three others who opted to drop geography and take the subject so the four of them had a huge room to themselves and it looked directly out over fields that swept away to far hills. He never wrote home about that class or that view because he knew no one would know what he was talking about.

After another year he was doing well and everyone was puzzled by his keenness and progress. He shrugged sheepishly when complimented and turned away to look into the distance. Miss Jack nurtured her prize pupil and never questioned his motives. There was a slight problem teaching and learning German in these times; all things German were suspect and alien. She was happy to have someone so keen on her own special subject.

In his third year the first few German prisoners started to arrive in the district and were sent to work in the fields. He met the ones sent to his farm and began gingerly to practise his elementary knowledge of their language. They smiled at each other and nodded, maybe because they were polite. They certainly didn't seem, what was that word, *belligerent* – yes, as in bellicose, warlike, as in

Caesar's bellicose wars, wasn't it? Something like that. Anyway, they didn't look a bit bellicose or belligerent, but rather like the team from another school come to get thrashed at cricket and knowing it beforehand and feeling it was going to happen and it did. And they began to reply to him at a speed that confounded, but he held on and made progress.

But the astonishing thing was that they seemed not much older than himself and looked as if they ought to have been lining up with him in school each morning as well as in the wheat and potato fields.

Watching his group of prisoners after the battle – or was it in the middle? You could never tell with a battle: it wasn't like a set piece or a football match where you have whistles to guide you and a time limit and breathers for drinks and injuries and time added on for stoppages. It all just happened and got muddled up together. Watching this group muddle up together and chat and smoke, Reevers thought he probably *hadn't* been here before after all.

They looked the same as the ones in his Shropshire fields – same age, same fair hair, same yellower skin – but the ones back home had been humble, lost almost, and that had made him go out of his way to be reasonable, friendly, and treat them as he would treat his classmates, offer them things, try to speak a bit of their language and sing some of their own songs to make them feel more at home, or less homesick maybe; and to make them feel that, war or no war, there was a way of behaving that was still beyond battle. But he felt different towards this lot. For someone who much preferred to drive and hold a steering wheel in his hand, he was glad he had his rifle now.

In his Shropshire school Miss Jack didn't just teach the

language, the grammar and vocabulary; she taught him about the customs and the community too, about German Christmases and beer-fests, about Tannenbaums and Maibaums, about Heine and Haydn and the romantic poems they wrote and the traditional songs they sang. She never talked about Hitler and Nazis, but about a Germany that seemed to exist or have existed outside of them, a Germany not associated with the Germany of the war but some separate land she knew well and was steeped in and in love with and could enrich her pupils with and about. Like a Northumberland before coal.

He learned songs like *Heidenröslein* and *Die Lorelei*, *Muss i denn* and *Kennst du das Land*; and when he was alongside the prisoners in the fields, he began to hum them, but at first got no response. They didn't recognise the tunes, or certainly not his version. When he had learned them better and felt more positive and they were beginning to converse with him because they were both getting over the accents, he tried again. Still there was no response. The young blond soldiers in the Shropshire fields simply stared, recognising their language, smiling at his attempts, but knowing nothing of what he was singing. And when in time he could begin to discuss with them he learned they had never known these pieces, never been taught them or heard them at their mothers' knee, because the Hitler youth never had time for such decadent and sentimental old songs, and they had been excised from the children's repertoire.

He couldn't comprehend that they knew nothing whatsoever of what he was singing, that they had never been taught their own riches, and Reevers thought that if he ever came out of the fields one day and went to war it might also be to show these youngsters the Germany of Miss Jack and to give them back their songs.

It sounded a daft reason and he wouldn't have dared mention it to anyone, even to Miss Jack, who would have understood of course but he was afraid to reveal too much of himself, let alone any weakness for the enemy because, since arriving from Northumberland, Reevers discovered he had had no desire to go to war. Others did. Weaned on the wondrous deeds of the *Wizard* and *Adventure*, and fired by the propaganda of films and magazines, covered with pictures of blazing aircraft and devastated desert tanks and stricken cargo ships, all of them German of course, most of his classmates could not wait to get out there and win medals for extraordinary deeds of daring beyond the call of duty and the screams of Germans being torn apart. They were all nurtured on tales of heroism on the wireless and in the comics and newspapers and from the rumours of war that came filtering back through to them in the fields and pubs and shops and classroom. Reevers preferred his horizons and his songs.

Unlike the prisoners in the Shropshire fields this group near Aachen seemed unaware of his presence. They were cold and miserable and presumably defeated. The Yanks had blown them out of their cover, messed up their offensive, shown them that the work they had done for von Runstedt, however magnificent, had all been in vain. The Bulge Battle was probably the last their nation could mount. They were now at the end of the road, or the beginning of the end of the road. But they were his prisoners, even if no one seemed to have informed them.

But if they had any thoughts on these lines, you wouldn't have detected them. They seemed insulated from the world he was living in, not part of what was happening yards away from them. Only their reaction to the cold assured Reevers that they were in the same world as he was. They seemed arrogant in their indifference, not just to Reevers but to their own plight. He wondered if they really knew what had happened to them, that they had been defeated, for Christ's sake! They must because of what they had been through and seen for themselves. You couldn't just walk out of a battlefield the way you emerged from a cinema and shrug off the feature behind you because the ending wasn't convincing. Experience like a battle couldn't be dropped and dismissed like a poor game of soccer. Yet they seemed to know, just as these boys in the Shropshire fields did, that it was all over and that no harm would come to them now. Despite the reports Major Bennett had been telling him about on the way down, about atrocities and offences against the Geneva Convention, that in their last desperate bid to salvage something out of the disastrous mess they had plunged the world and themselves into, the Germans were no longer acting in accordance with *any* rules of war, among this group there seemed neither interest nor concern, responsibility nor regret, not even disappointment or anxiety, or any of the other weaknesses you would have expected them to show with the odds stacked against them as they were. These young men were simply a group of soldiers who had paused for a smoke and a chat before continuing their victorious progress.

Reevers felt very uneasy with his thoughts and tucked the butt of his rifle into his side. Then he was OK again. He wished the GIs would hurry along. He knew they had been through a bad time and were recuperating over there, through the trees, across the roadway, milling around their huts and tanks and trucks, but surely they could spare a couple of their own men to look after their own prisoners. Well, it was the major's doing, really. He had spotted the prisoners and heard the shouts for a guard to take over and had volunteered Reevers. Maybe to make an impression, like compensating for not having been down here in the first place and taking some of the load. Nice enough bloke, the major, but officers were like that, and sometimes when they got together they chatted about the jolly old war as if it were just another Saturday game with them standing wrapped up in scarves on the touchline shouting advice and not really bothered about who won anyway as long as it was a ripping good scrap. And offering Reevers to the Yanks to guard a dozen prisoners was like offering him to the visiting team to look after their supporters while they had a pint after the game.

It probably was to impress the Yanks too that the major could boast a driver who could 'get his tongue around a bit of the old deutsch'. Only there were twelve of them and one of him! Funny blokes, officers.

And yet twelve to one it was. If they wanted to they could easily . . . Rubbish, he told himself, the US army was only a snowball away across the ditch. They'd never dare. Besides, they seemed completely uninterested. He felt easier in mind but not in body, and the thick slab of wood and steel pressed into him seemed a part of his frame.

For something of the same reason Reevers had not gone home to see his family in Ashington. He had a new life that he didn't want to give up, not even to be a hero in a war that was as far away now as the chimneys and pit heaps and black and rain and smog and traffic of his other life. It was *another* life. It was as if he had never known any other. Now that he had tasted this one he wanted it and he wanted it always and had no need or desire to go back to his origins. They say blood is thicker than water but he doubted that now. It seemed another of these old wives' tales or clichés you got in Patience Strong poems in the weekend papers.

He had pangs of conscience of course, great waves of the stuff that would surge over him during the early mornings when he awoke to the calls of birds and animals and sat up abruptly in bed to look out and confirm the horizon was still there and thought of the rain and the gaslight and the smell of coal fire and bacon frying. He felt terribly disloyal.

But it was what his blood was doing to him, what his body was feeling. This thicker than water business, what did it mean? The blood that was thickening for him these days had nothing to do with families. And even if he had wanted to be loyal, it could only have been at the cost of denying something else, something to do with blood stirring, yes, but the horizons too, all sorts of horizons, not just the ones with the sheep. Everything he touched and looked at now seemed to have a separate horizon; everything that was happening inside him had to do with horizons, fuzzy ones, admittedly, but horizons.

He truly wanted to be left there for all his life, and if long ago in darkest Northumberland he had once had some idea of fighting for freedom it had all gone from him and he had no wish to uproot himself from these golden fields and troop off to Germany or wherever to fight for something he wasn't interested in. When he looked back at these 'coal years' as he was calling them, which he didn't do very much now, he felt as if he had fought his corner, done his bit and penance, and now he had been rewarded. In Shropshire he had already been demobbed from one war. Not another, thank you. I've done my time. And it wasn't his mind that was telling him these things, but his body, and that thicker blood they kept talking about.

Now as this new line of flaxen-haired shot-through, blue-eyed youngsters crouched chatting and thumping their shoulders to keep warm and exchanging cigarettes quite oblivious to the outside world, either of his own nervous menace or the hustle and rumble of GIs and their machines across the ditch, Reevers wondered: is this another group similarly deprived of fields and horizons; is their preoccupation with themselves and their isolation from the world outside the pall of icy breath and tobacco smoke that hung around them like a protective net an easy acceptance that, like the Shropshire lads, it was all over for them, it happened long ago, and they were neither hurt nor bothered? Like injured players on the touchline, were they simply out of the game? Whatever, *their* blood must have its thickening properties too.

Reevers had read that the losers in battle are always sunken and dejected; and the wounded on the losing side always the ones to heal the slowest. But these men, or boys, seemed to have no interest in anything outside their pall of smoke. They were neither despondent nor relieved. They seemed to have no interest or concern beyond the subject matter of their own chatter which, as far as he could glean through the bewildering mixture of accents he had never heard in Miss Jack's class in Weaveney, concerned only beer and cigarettes and women. Never war. Neither the last battle nor their coming fate.

Beer, cigarettes and women. And above all, women. They seemed to know a lot about women, a helluva lot more than he did; and they didn't seem a day older. And it wasn't only jokes about women, the kind of raucous stories you heard at home, in the fields, in the pubs, in the classroom even, certainly in the barrack room when he had joined up. That had really shocked him out of his dream world, took him back to Northumberland in a way, not because of what they said but because of the darkness of it.

It was the only real subject of masculine interest: what you did with women, or to them; what you wanted to do to them, what they needed, what they needed to have done to them, what they deserved, what they had coming to them; in fact what they were here *for*. He was desperately unsure but he went along with it all – the laughs, that is. He had to.

But with these young Germans, it wasn't like that at all. They were sharing their experiences. Coldly exchanging tales and comparing encounters and performances. The difference seemed to be that what he had always heard back home consisted of hopes, wishes, desires, boasts, *desperate* boasts, but never achievements. Here, it seemed that these young men like himself had only ever achieved, as if they had never ever had to try or wonder, as if they belonged to a quite different form of society and mode of behaviour. The eternal wishful thinking of Reevers' compatriots seemed to be permanent fulfilment in theirs. There was no mystery for them. And he wondered if there ever had been.

Although he grasped only the nub of their chat, Reevers stood astonished, not noticing how his feet were freezing through inaction. Only once did he catch an eye, a glance, from one of them, but it was accidental. They had no idea he was listening, *could* listen. In fact he thought they would not have been the slightest interested if they had been told he knew every word. Their conversation like their war was open. They had concluded a chapter in their lives and were not going either to re-read it or analyse it. Reevers was reminded of half-time in a compulsory football game at school when you all clustered around and talked of what you would be doing that night, never the game in hand: the first half was past, the second would come anyway; in the meantime you looked forward to more important things.

All the same he kept his rifle cocked and pointed, and the very indifference and isolation of this band made him press the butt more firmly into his side.

The single glance brought him out of his reverie and

he felt his feet ice cold and rooted. He moved them and began to clump to and fro.

When Reevers and Bennett had driven up, the scene looked like a circus or fairground. The tree-lined roadway led to a clearing with a few houses and huts, a petrol station and a shop. On either side of the main road the landscape opened on to fields and copses. Reevers thought of the last few miles as a dark tunnel which suddenly ended in brightness caused by daylight and snow, like his own journey from enclosing coal to opening fields.

The place was littered with the paraphernalia of war, machinery and men scattered all about, like a fairground that has just arrived and spread out its gear to be checked out and maintained before erecting. Men swarmed everywhere, mostly GIs but Germans too. No one seemed to notice which was which. They were chatting and lounging, smoking and drinking, examining, stamping feet in the snow, slapping arms around shoulders. No one was giving any orders. They were simply sorting themselves out, idling, stretching, breathing, like footballers at half time when it's too far to go back to the pavilion.

Their arrival raised no interest. Major Bennett jumped down and bustled around as if he was quite certain he was being expected. But it took him some time to locate whoever he was here to meet. No one seemed to know or be interested. Reevers dutifully hung around his wagon watching the chaotic scene and thought that if it had been back at his place everyone would have been polishing something by now. The atmosphere here was completely different. He liked it. It was a mess but no one was pretending otherwise – just getting on with the surprise of still being alive.

And when Major Bennett turned up with the American officer and made his suggestion about the prisoners, it seemed laughable. They looked completely happy and harmless as they were. In fact the Yanks had not even got around to noticing them. But the fussy major had, so that meant something had to be done. That was the thing about British officers: always searching for something for their men to do, in case they were incapable of doing nothing. His mother had a proverb about that, something to do with idle hands. He had never been allowed to enjoy the experience of doing nothing.

So now he had to heave himself away from the bonnet of his truck and the much more interesting pastime of watching the behaviour of the Yanks whom he had never met before, and hump off with his posse of bored German youngsters to a copse on the other side of the road where he was to 'guard' them, for Christ's sake and Major Bennett's, in case of what he had no idea, because they were unarmed and doing absolutely nothing until the major intervened and they were quite bewildered at being disturbed. It was a gesture from the Yanks that they paid any attention to Major Bennett at all, but presumably once he had pointed out the 'problem' of unarmed enemy doing nothing, they had to do something. So Reevers trudged off the long twenty yards through the snow with his rifle and charges, pondering this latest display of mindless authority.

Now, standing in the smell and dust and filth and stench and din of battle, watching what looked to be the same group of youngsters he had worked with before, he wondered why they were fighting each other instead of getting on with their harvests, and if it had been left to him and the others at home, they probably wouldn't have gone to war for whatever it was they disagreed about, not when it meant this smell and dust and filth and stench and din and freezing indifference and desperation and tearing bodies apart instead of the heroic dying you got in the *Hotspur*.

He had not been too sure why he was going; four years

with the German language and Miss Jack's devotion, and
two years working with live Germans had convinced him
there is always a nagging doubt about certainties. Maybe,
had he been left to rot in the north-east pits and the boot
had been on the other foot, *they* might have come to
rescue him when they thought about what he had been
deprived of.

Twice a GI came to check and pass on a message from
Major Bennett that they would be heading back soon. But
he must have reported that he appeared content and was
enjoying his vigil with his smart attempts at German and
whistling weird tunes, so they left him to it.

Maybe he *was* enjoying it. In a way. It was the first
time since he joined up that he had been given any
responsibility, guarding a group of Germans, and not
because he had a rifle but because the major had said:
'leave them to my driver, Reevers. Handy with the old
German, Reevers.' He became a driver because he had
been driving a tractor since he was fourteen and didn't
need much training. Not many chaps of his age had a
licence and he must have been one of the few men to
whom the Army ever gave the job they could do best in
civvy street. He liked driving: 'Gets you about.'

Another thing about these trips: the ordinary British
squaddy stays put with his own kind and fights the
war from one fixed perspective. Driving you get out
and about a bit. His spoken German really wasn't up
to much, but it had got him closer to something else
again. Can't be bad.

He wondered if he ought to try whistling a few bars,
and gingerly, casually, offered a touch of *Heidenröslein*,
but nothing happened. Then *Die Lorelei*, but they didn't
bat an eyelid. He dug out a few more and turned up the
volume, but nothing. It wasn't as if he was addressing

them in a bad German they could be forgiven for not recognising. Music was different. But no. And when he told them in German not to huddle too close, they did respond, recognising some of the words, but without a flicker of interest, as if theirs was the only language on earth anyway and they would expect any English lout with a Lee Enfield entrusted with the responsibility of guarding them to know it. But they didn't know their own songs.

Driving got him some good numbers, like this trip. He hadn't met the Yanks before and was glad to get down to their sector and have a look and listen. He didn't mingle but saw enough to know they were different. More rough and tumble, more casual. Less bull, too. As he waited for the major, he watched them hustling about and shouting and joking and smoking and generally being at ease, despite the belting they had taken.

They were at ease with their officers too. That startled him. There didn't seem to be any real distance between the officers and the sergeants and other ranks and none of the rigid coming to attention and saluting every time they got within a mile of one. No barrack square stomping around that distinguished all British squaddies. None of the strutting among the officers as if class and rank defined one's gait as well. All Yanks shuffled rather than stomped or strutted.

They lounged too. 'Slouch' was the word he usually heard used about them. Yet there was an energy in it. He got a buzz. It wasn't the same as Major Bennett's energy when he had fussed around looking for hapless German prisoners to do things to, always on the move, whacking thighs with batons. The American energy seemed there without effort while people like the major had to muster it up to show others they were different.

He had been warned the Yanks had no discipline and

that was their trouble. Trouble? He couldn't see what trouble. They looked battle-worn and care-worn and tired and roughed up. The reports said they had fought well. Their difference in attitude hadn't seemed to alter their ability to fight. They had come a long way since Normandy and had carried the brunt of the attack, and now the counter-attack too. Trouble?

This time he sang a few words of *Heidenröslein* and *Die Lorelei*. It worked. They were momentarily intrigued, but there was no recognition. Only that the words were German. He tried again: *In einem kühlen Grunde* and *Muss i denn*. Recognition to a point, yes, but interest, no. He had been right. They really didn't know. His journey here had been worthwhile; and he thought of their counterparts in Shropshire. Ironic, he was out here on behalf of these chaps at home, and now here was another bunch they might be sending back. And he was fighting – well, driving – to win back their songs for them while they lounged in his fields! Bizarre, that's what war was. Well, at least he knew why he was here, he thought, stretching, thumping the butt into his side, and that was the important thing.

No sign yet either of Major Bennett or relief. He was cold, and bored now, and on that impulse walked around the group and looked down at them.

Imagine, no roots! Denied their own bloody songs! What kind of people were doing this to them? What they had done to destroy *his* childhood was bad enough, but at least he had been lucky enough to escape. Any difference from what had happened to this lot swapping yarns about women in the snow?

They had been denied too.

Now here he was, 'guarding' this group because some fuss-pot of a major had thought he needed something to do and that they should be kept out of 'mischief'; and thinking he had given up his beloved fields to fight them to give them back their songs! What a load of old cobblers!

Buggering about with other men's youth: that's what the war was about; that's what he was doing here!

The three German tanks materialised, stray pieces, emerging bewildered from the dark of the woods, the watery sun on their bared muzzles as if blinking in the unexpected light, taken aback at finding a whole unit of the US Army standing easy, probably unaware the battle was over and the rest of their army gone.

Before the scattered groups could register something alien had arrived, the guns opened up and swept their shells and bullets over the busy scene. Men and machines were thrust into the air, flung to all sides, and dumped contemptuously in the snow.

The foreground troops, relaxing, repairing, tidying up, took the brunt and the casualties, and it was some time before their covering tanks and artillery could muster themselves into action. When they did, the Germans fared badly. They were isolated, on a lone sortie, unaware they were not so much cut off from their main army as abandoned by it. And they were only three. But odds on or against, for minutes they were ruthless, devastating masters of their scene.

Reevers saw his truck ripped apart and fall in on the road like a drunk whose legs have given way. In the copse he and his group of prisoners were dazzled and dumbfounded as men were torn apart before their eyes, tossed in the air like rag dolls in a children's game.

From their privileged position, they looked on transfixed, astounded spectators in a theatre box mesmerised by the illusionist. And in his wonder, in 'the chaos of battle', as they say, Reevers' prisoners made their break.

*   *   *

'Can't say I really blame them,' said Major Archie Bennett when he made his report the following morning. 'That's their job.'

'Nice bloke too,' said someone in the mess. 'Used to drive for me.'

'All the same', said the major, wisely, 'relaxing in battle, you know – *and* with prisoners!'

Back at Reevers' unit, the story expanded: 'Had 'em all huddled around singing songs to keep 'em warm, the major said.'

'Not very nice of them, though. I mean, they were *their* songs.'

HOLY WATERS

Xanten, The Rhine, March 1945

Eight

At dusk on the night of 23rd March, as he watched the final preparations for the assault on the Rhine and listened to the cursing troops of the Fifteenth Scottish Division of the Second British Army manoeuvring their machines into position for a midnight crossing, Alabaster said, 'I don't like the feel of this. We shouldn't be tampering with this.' And he spread out his arms to indicate the world gathering around the quiet river.

Alabaster Simcott was pale. Pale as an unglazed pot. Appropriate for him. He came from Stoke, one of the five pottery towns Arnold Bennett wrote about. 'Plain grey, or plane grey, with brown tippings'.

His real name was Alasdair – 'from his mother's side' – which accounted for him serving with the Fifteenth Scottish: 'With a name like that you ought to be in a kilt', said the recruiting officer; and for the rest of the war, which wasn't long in Alasdair's case as he was called up six months before it ended, he had been with the Jocks who refused to call him Alasdair because of his accent, and dubbed him Alabaster instead because of his pasty complexion, or rather 'yon clay look'.

Alabaster had been brought up in pots. His father, who never got further than the furnace of Tobruk in 1941, had been a pottery worker all his life, like his father before

him who had been fired in Mesopotamia in 1916. He had
met his wife in a Musselburgh factory when delivering
a consignment of unpainted ware which she had been
hired to paint thistles on – 'so clay was in the blood'.
It was love at first sight and she had eloped with him
from the raw breezes of the Forth to the clogged airs of
the Black Country. Alasdair was born into a world and a
house of pots and wheels because both mother and father
worked in the factory by day and ran their own little
business at home in the evenings and at weekends.

'There's something eerie about this,' said Alabaster to
Sergeant Macintyre of Musselburgh as they stopped to
survey the river lying placidly below them. 'I mean, it's
not ours, is it? Not with all them Lorelies and things.
More like the Ganges.'

Everyone was crossing the Rhine that spring. It was
the in-thing in army travel now that the lure of desert
oases and the charms of the Italian Riviera had worn
off.

The Americans started it at Remagen on 7th March
and the French wound it up at Strasbourg over a
month later on 15th April. In between there were no
fewer than another twenty-two crossings, fourteen by
the Americans, three by the British, and five by the
French. But they came after all the others had been and
gone and done it.

'Cooks could have made a fortune here,' said Sergeant
Macintyre of Musselburgh, staring across and contemplating how many men he had to ship over for the night's
assault.

The names of the crossing points rang like a Wag-
nerian recital: Oppenheim, Nierstein, Buderich, Rheinberg, Boppard, Rhens, Oberwesel, Frankenthal, Mainz,
a long Germanic litany that seemed to emerge from
mists of legends and folklore, and from echoes of things

tribal and mystical, of memories from the blood, not the brain and the page. Literature came later, much later, in a civilised effort to capture on paper the meaning of these intangible things. But they were a poorer substitute. You heard it in the ring of the words, words that came from voices, not pages; and you felt it in the air, air that seemed to hover above the worldly blasphemies and the calls of christless invocations from Scottish soldiers, as if reminding them that their efforts were material and limited and finite, whereas whatever they thought they were conquering or achieving or destroying was beyond all that, arrogantly distanced from their puny labours. In a word, sacred. And that was Alabaster's problem: the sacredness of the Rhine. It didn't matter that the battles had to be won, the bridges saved or rebuilt, the amphibian craft revved up and ready to go, while armies padded impatiently along the river banks waiting to get over and get on and get it done with and get home. What mattered was that they were there at all, like locusts plaguing the acres of something sacred. Alabaster wanted no part of it. It didn't matter that there had already been eight crossings and there might be as many as a dozen more to come. What mattered was that he was there and he was to do it: tamper with someone else's holy waters.

'You can't meddle with things like this,' he was saying. 'Nothing to do with Nazis. Goes back a lot further than all of them.'

They were solitary people, the Simcotts, if you can call three of them solitary. And they were only interested in pots. Pots and pottery. Alabaster was fourteen when war broke out and his dad forty.

It all happened so quickly. One minute Jeff Simcott

was standing behind his young son holding his delicate uncoordinated hands and guiding them around
a splodge of clay on his home potter's wheel, and
the next he was sending postcards home from sunny
Tobruk; although, being mysterious like all potters, he
never actually wrote 'Tobruk', only told them that he
was holidaying at a place with a babbling brook and
enclosing yellow grains in the envelope.

But the heat got to him and he was shipped home
to convalesce and never got around to going back, by
which time Shotton and Greaves had changed over to
manufacturing for the war effort, and the production of
fine cups, saucers and plates had been ended. Instead
had come the massive demand for plain – 'very plain'
– crockery for the armed forces: 'Naafi weaponry'.

Unrefined earthenware – white, thick, cumbersome,
'the nearest we can make to unbreakable'. Noble,
dependable ware that had the look of institutional
austerity and offered to the artists in the Potteries the
only consolation possible: that 'our crocks are helping
to smash Hitler'.

'We should try dropping some of this on Dresden,'
Jeff Simcott observed ruefully as he visited his old
workplace and tried to break some of the 'seconds' that
emerged from the kilns. 'If it doesn't break their heads,
it should break their bleeding hearts.' They became
factory sayings at Shotton and Greaves: 'Another load
for Dresden then?' Or: 'This should go down well in
Dresden, eh?' Or: 'If you think this is rough, just think
of the poor buggers in Dresden?' Or when it was really
rough and unforgivably leaden: 'I wouldn't drop that
on my worst enemy in Dresden.'

Alabaster's dad now found himself in a reserved
occupation instead, up and about in time to take part
in the big change-over to manufacturing 'hush-hush'
equipment for the War Office.

'You're needed here, Simcott,' said Mr Marples with suitable wartime gravity. 'We have been commandeered to produce special equipment.'

'WCs for the Naafi, is it?' asked Jeff. 'Or wash-basins, admirals, for the use of?'

'No need to be cynical, Simcott. Most men would give their right arms to be free from action.'

'On the Dresden line, then, Mr Marples? Special dinner services for Bomber Command, is it?'

'No, they do that better at Harleys. It's electrical porcelain.'

'Oh, high-voltage bricks, is it?'

'Not exactly.'

'Oh, I'm disappointed. So what's it, then, porcelain insulators, chips for power lines? Sparking plugs for the PM's Rolls?'

'Slightly more refined than that. For radio and radar instruments, actually.'

'Well, I suppose that's as near Dresden as we'll get, Mr Marples.'

'In more ways than one, yes.'

The Rhine was quiet that night. Or Alabaster thought it was. Rivers were silent by nature. But not troops, and especially not troops of the Fifteenth Scottish Division. The assault was set for the early hours of the following morning – 'midnight plus' – as if some surprise purpose had been built in. If so the Higher Command had mistakenly calculated on the silence of the troops detailed to cross at Xanten.

In the rare lulls between the curses of men and the creaks of machinery Alabaster found himself straining for a snatch of a note from the waters that seemed to be edging indifferently past the great activity going on along its west banks. He cupped his ears as if to catch a snip of the silence in between the uproar of men manipulating their trucks and machines and landing craft and Buffaloes and half-tracks and stormboats.

Funny that. Listening to a river. What can you hear except the water moving? If the water isn't disturbed by man or wind, what can you possibly hear? What is the sound of water, if it isn't the sound of lapping along or around an object? Does it have its own sound, the sound of itself? Alabaster tensed himself and strained to catch a snatch of the river: the tune, the theme, the measure. But what is the measure of a river? he went on. And more immediate, what is the measure of the *Rhine*?

Alabaster had a thing about things. Eerie things. Ghost things. Things that didn't add up. Not God things, but *before* God things. Something before even *He* arrived. Like H.G. Wells and all that other space stuff in *The War of the Worlds*, *The Time Machine*, *The First Men in the Moon*, *The Food of the Gods*. Alabaster had read them all. And *Mr Polly*. He felt it. 'Then we come along with all our wars and troubles, and disturb it,' he said aloud to the Allies. 'But this thing's been here a lot longer than that, you know.'

Jeff and Madge Simcott went out together each day to help in the porcelain war effort and were fortunate to be able to nurture their only child on the finer skills of their craft. They were determined that because they had been given a lucky break from war service, they would use it to keep alive the true potter's spirit throughout the war years, even if only in one boy, and that when the young Alasdair finally came out into the adult world after the war, his skills would be developed and the tradition would be intact, the continuity unbroken.

In the evenings, between shifts and at weekends, they taught him the skills and tricks of the trade and gave him a sense of his place in the scheme of pottery 'and all art things'. 'Remember, son, pottery is only an extended form of poetry. Only an extra T separates them.'

They taught him about Greek pottery and how the Greeks made vases in red and black by heating iron oxide in smoky instead of clear fires. They taught him how tin oxide added to a glaze makes it white and transparent. They taught him how the Moors brought it to Spain and then on to Italy and to France. And how in Holland it became Delft and around the beginning of the eighteenth century moved to England. And they taught him how the Chinese used kaolin, a pure form of clay that turned pure white when fired. And when they mixed it with petuntse it became hard and glasslike and came to be called porcelain.

And they taught him about Sèvres and Meissen, Bow and Chelsea, Derby and Worcester, and Wedgwood and their own Staffordshire. Alasdair took it all in and silently absorbed most of the techniques and not a little of the mystery. Mr Marples knew of his progress and prowess and invited him to the factory occasionally to see how they did things there, apologising for the 'heavy duty' stuff they had had to commit themselves to 'during these dark days' but assuring him that the future was 'full of promise' and that one day when he returned from doing his 'duty for King and Country' he would be welcomed back like a hero and would find a warm place for himself beside the kilns of 'the noble family of Shotton and Greaves' and take his 'rightful place' in the 'long and hallowed tradition' of pots and clay.

Alasdair had not liked the factory atmosphere at all and much preferred the quiet wheel in his own home, but he said nothing as his mother and father were obviously delighted that their son would 'come into

such an inheritance' one day. Nor could he understand
the bit about being welcomed back as a hero as he
had never considered going anywhere anyway. He
kept quiet about that too, sensing that his mother
and father wanted him to be the hero his dad had
been so cruelly prevented from being. But what his
dad had said about Tobruk was good enough for him.
And above all he kept quiet about the fact that he could
never understand why his mother and father worked
each day and all day and often well into the night
to make tiny little sections of white porcelain to help
defeat the people who made Dresden.

'Well, springtime is bridge time,' said Alabaster to
Sergeant Macintyre of Musselburgh, looking down
miserably at the herculean efforts the Fifteenth were
making to get their landing craft into position at Xanten
and trying to listen to something in the clear March air
that was more reminiscent of the Rhine in all its glory,
of its legends and maidens and myths and sagas, than
the contrasting chorus of orchestrated blasphemy that
accompanied the efforts of his minor men below.

'Of course, Heine might have thought it poetry too,
you know,' he observed as the chorus of curses wound
their way up the banks. 'You can never tell if you don't
know the language, can you?'

Sergeant Macintyre of Musselburgh shrugged. They
studied another heave on a stubborn Buffalo and
listened for the distant obscenities to ring out their
cheer like ancient tribal taunts to the enemy on the
other side.

'I'm not sure you need ammunition with this kind
of assault,' said Alabaster. 'These bloodcurdling epi-
thets would be enough to make *me* scarper. Why are
these men always *played* into battle with their pipes,
Sergeant? The skirl of their language seems powerful

enough to me. With it you get the double effect of music *and* battlecry. They could keep their pipes for afters, you know, to celebrate when they've done the job.'

'Could they now?' Sergeant Macintyre of Mussel-burgh contributed.

When Alasdair got his papers at Christmas 1944 his mother and father were shocked. Despite all their dreams of Alasdair becoming their heroic son, a nobil-ity of achievement that would sit well with his pottery skills that were assuredly blossoming into an art, they had not expected the war to last that long. In a way they hadn't really noticed, so concentrated were they on their porcelain radar pieces and their son's enrichment. They would miss the medal, of course, and the plaudits of adulation, but now they would much prefer that he had been robbed of his chance.

'Well, it's nearly over anyway, Dad,' said Alasdair, who was by now quite philosophical. 'It's the clay, see. Makes you think of denser things.'

Jeff Simcott said, 'That's what we said at Tobruk. But there's not much chance of sunstroke in Europe.'

'Well, they'll be in Berlin before I even get through basic training.'

'Maybe.'

'Besides. We're lucky.'

'Lucky!'

'Well, no offence, mind. But you could have been gone for four years at least. That's luck, isn't it?'

'Well . . .'

'Besides. It's our turn.'

'Whose?'

'Ours. Mine. I mean, your lot fought the first part, didn't they? Well, your *kind*, I mean. All that Dunkirk and Desert stuff. That was your quota, so to speak. Now, it's up to us younger lads to go and complete what you started.'

'Huh, never thought of it that way,' said Jeff. 'But it's such a waste. You, and all your skills!'

'I can bring them back. Besides, they make me doubly lucky, don't they? I got them. Many people don't.'

'I mean . . . if . . . oh, never mind.'

'I don't, Dad.'

'Something mysterious in pots,' Alasdair said on the road up to Xanten. The company had halted for a brew-up amidst a pile of rubble that had once been a village and Alasdair had wandered into the ruins of a house where he found a pair of cups strangely preserved in what had once been someone's kitchen. As the others slurped their tea out in the raw March air, Alasdair stood in the kitchen chaos turning the delicate pieces over and over in his hands.

'Mind if I come in?' said Sergeant Macintyre of Musselburgh, standing on the rubble of what had once been a threshold to the entrance of what had once been a kitchen.

Preoccupied with his cups, Alasdair said absently, 'No, please do.' And he stumbled back through the debris as if moving aside to let him in. 'Sorry about the mess.'

'Don't worry,' said Sergeant Macintyre, 'I know how difficult it is to get the staff these days. But I hope I'm not messing your carpet, am I?' he added, dustily stamping dust off his dust-laden boots in the dust of the kitchen.

Alasdair remained absorbed. He held the cups as if picking up cobwebs.

'What you got yourself there then, pal?' asked Sergeant Macintyre of Musselburgh, slurping tea from a scorched can.

Alasdair extended the cups gingerly.

'Oh, great,' said the sergeant, 'bout time we had our char out of something civilised for a change.'

'It's Meissen, Sergeant,' Alabaster whispered. 'Genuine Meissen.'

'Well, we're no fussy, like you, Simcott.'

'But, Sergeant,' said Alabaster, at last tuning in to what the sergeant was implying. 'They're . . . precious. We can't use them for tea!'

The sergeant slurped and said, 'So, what you thinking of using them for then – porridge?'

'No,' Alabaster held the cups in his palms as if they were sparrow's eggs about to break at any moment and prove their life. 'I mean, there's something . . .' but he could only stare and shake his head in admiration and for lack of words.

'Go on, then,' the sergeant chivvied him. 'Finish what ye have to say, man! We've got a ferry to catch, remember.'

Challenged, Alabaster came alive. In defence of his precious pots, his subservience and silence disappeared. Taking off his beret he placed it at his feet between two bricks and delicately nestled one of the two cups in the woollen cradle. Then he stretched and held up the second cup to the light as if to look through it. Sergeant Macintyre of Musselburgh peered with him.

'See?' he asked.

'No,' said the sergeant.

'It's almost transparent.'

'Ah, well, if I want tae see the colour of my tea I usually look doon anyway. Not much point looking through the side unless you're a bairn, is there?'

But Alabaster was elsewhere. After a few seconds of turning the cup to and fro, groping for the right angle to see it through the dense dust floating overhead, he lowered the cup covered in particles and breathed on it.

'You thinking on polishing it?' asked the sergeant.

'No,' said Alabaster, 'but you can blow too hard, you know.' He snuggled it in his palms, then said, 'It's the shapes that come oozing up between your fingers as the clay spins, see?' And amid the rubbled kitchen, he began to improvise a demonstration by placing his thumbs inside the bowl and turning the cup between his palms while the slurping of boiling tea from the sergeant's stained can added a counterpointing musical accompaniment as in a documentary film. 'You shape it without knowing what you are shaping,' his commentary went. 'Like Venus emerging from the sea, see.'

Less noisily now the sergeant toned down from a slurp to a sip and said, 'Oh aye,' non-committally, while Alabaster pressed on desperate to stay off the execution and yet carried away to another time and experience.

'Well, she did, and it does,' he went on nervously, continuing to fondle the cup and mould it around in his palms and put his fingers inside and draw them around and up to the rim and on again, reproducing the movement of the potter's hands. 'It's all part of the same mystery.'

'But of course,' Sergeant Macintyre of Musselburgh agreed, and blew gently on the surface of his tea.

'Well, who knows, son,' said Jeff Simcott at Stoke-on-Trent station the night Alasdair embarked for Germany. 'You might even reach Dresden yet and see it all for yourself.'

'Never thought of that.'

'I might envy you now. Not a lot of china at Tobruk.'

'Think there'll be anything left by the time I get there, Dad?'

'Well, if there is, fetch us back a bit, will you?'

'Do my best.'

'Wish I could offer you something to take with you. But I don't suppose they'd give a deutchsmark for any of our stuff.'

'Don't worry. I'll think of something, Dad.'

'That's the mystery, see?' Alabaster was fighting for his life.

'No.' Slurp. The sip had moved up an octave again.

'Water and clay, see?'

'No exactly.' Slurp. 'But do go on, Mr Simcott.'

'It's all about men shaping their first implements and figures of worship.'

'Ah, well now, if you'd only said.'

Alabaster felt himself returning to a world of his own by the effect on his fingers of the two precious pieces of china, transmitting to him something of their energy and history and inspiring him to sing their praises and pass on something of their hallowedness, and so to defend them in their hour of danger.

'They shouldn't have survived here, Sergeant Macintyre. Not *here*.' And he turned with a cup in each hand to sweep his arms around the pile of devastated bricks and stones and charred wood that had once combined to form a room, a house, and a home. 'It's like finding two children still alive in the ruins.'

'No the kind A've got, Simcott – all grub and glaur even after half an hour in the kirk.'

Alasdair looked back down at the delicate cups. 'They're priceless . . .'

'Are you wanting them as spoils of war, is that it?' said Sergeant Macintyre of Musselburgh. 'Are you asking me to condone downright *pillage*, is that your game?'

'No, Sergeant,' Alasdair pleaded. 'I only wanted to preserve them for themselves. There are things that we have to preserve, even in war, you know.'

'I didn't. But go on.'

Alabaster looked around again at the smouldering ruins as if trying to reshape it in his mind's eye. 'The fact that they survived all this has a meaning.'

'That's deep, Simcott. Ho, that's very deep, so it is!'

'It tells us something.'

Sergeant Macintyre of Musselburgh took a last slurp. 'It tells *me* it's time to get moving,' he said. 'And if you want my opinion', he added, spraying the dregs around the smouldering rubble, 'it's plain bloody looting, whatever fancy names you want to give it.'

'Sergeant, I swear, if their owners were here now, I would return them to them.' And surveying again the whole pulverised village, he added, 'But they're gone. And I doubt they will return. To leave them would be to abandon them.'

Sergeant Macintyre of Musselburgh squinted and studied Alabaster for a few seconds. Then, 'You're a queer wee bugger, Simcott, so you are,' he said. 'But you've got something tucked away behind that mealy look of yours, although I haven't got the time to put my finger on it right now. I've got a ferry to catch.'

In the truck on the last road to the Rhine, Sergeant Macintyre demanded, 'So, tell me about the mystery, Mr Simcott.' They were squeezed together in the front cabin, Alabaster wedged up to the driver and entangled with the gear levers, while Sergeant Macintyre tried to spread his hulk evenly over the rest of the seat and out of the window.

Alabaster stared ahead aware that one slip, one hesitation, one unconvincing argument, and his precious pair of cups might end up in the general mess crockery. He took a deep breath and, rigidly staring ahead to concentrate as if defending his own life, he said without a pause, 'If you stand all your life at a potter's wheel, and watch the land and the water coming up through your hands, you feel the power of the universe in the dirt of your finger nails. You have the great white sun in your hands and the great brown earth in your fingers and you watch earth and water forming and you shaping the world, or the world coming into shape through your fingers, and the whole block turning around like the movement of the spheres and the stars and the planets.'

The driver changed down and then down again. The noise cut out Alabaster's soliloquy. They bumped over hunks of shattered concrete and prayed they had avoided the rusted rods of reinforcing sticking menacingly through. They swung around a lumbering tank and headed on towards two Bren carriers, halted because of burnt-out tyres. The driver gave a quick glance towards the sergeant still wedged half through the window but without so much as a glance the sergeant said, 'Keep going, Ross!' Yards later, still without turning, he said, 'You were saying, Mr Simcott?'

On cue, the tensed-up Alabaster took another breath and continued, 'So, when you get as close to the water and the soil as I have been, then you think differently. You've got your hands on the earth, and the great world in your hands. You've got to keep on shaping it or wetting it, take its shape through you, because that's what it means when it says in the great book that we were made in his image and that, no matter what we are doing, we are always trying to recreate that image whether making clay or hay or music. We are all doing the same thing, trying to make sense and a symphony of it.'

They thundered on past more debris and swerved to avoid another broken-down carrier. They raised more dust and showered a platoon of troops trundling along laden with full kit who looked forlornly up at the truck as if their looks would qualify them for a lift. But the sergeant never noticed and said, 'Keep going, Ross!' And the driver changed down and revved up again and they could see the line of the Rhine ahead.

'So, you were saying, Mr Simcott?'

'So you have to be careful when you interfere with other men's symbols and effigies and idols and icons.'

'Dear Son,' Jeff Simcott wrote.

'We have no idea where you are now but wherever that is we hope it finds you well and happy given the circumstances of your journey and that you are not being required to do any heavy manual work that might endanger the delicacy of those precious fingers of yours. Whatever else you do you must make sure they come back with you. There's not much I can advise you about Europe I'm afraid it not being a part of the world of which I have much first-hand knowledge and I don't have many contacts over your way. Had it been the Desert of course it would have been a different matter and I might have been able to put you in touch with a few chaps in Tobruk but it isn't and as we all know things don't always work out according to plan do they so that's another story by now. So all I can say is that we are fine here, pottering along as usual and your mum's keeping fine and Mr Marples too always telling us he's keeping your place warm by the old Shotton and Greaves kiln. I don't suppose you will have much chance to keep up with your career out there but you never know and of course if you do get to Dresden don't forget the souvenir.'

'My mother came from Musselburgh, Sergeant,' said Alabaster as the truck pulled up and they looked down on the Rhine.

'Poor bitch.'

'She did, you know. Said she never stopped feeling homesick.'

The sergeant looked out over the calm waters, taking in his next challenge, sizing up the new opposition. This was a big one. The Rhine was big. And the task to get across that night even bigger. He needed a moment with himself to size up his enemy. He always surveyed his enemy quietly first, a few moments of private reflection taking in the whole scene before coming to and then working out his tactics.

He sighed, cleared his throat and pulled himself together, then lowered his arm to open the door from the outside. Before pressing down the handle, he turned to Alabaster, 'Don't ever try buttering me up, Simcott. You want to nick a pair of cups, then you nick em.' He leaned over to meet Alabaster's eyes. 'Or if you have to ask my permission first, ask me straight.'

'Yes, Sergeant.'

He lowered himself out of the truck and turned back. 'And don't ever try that mealy-mouthed shite on me again, see?'

'Dear Son,' Jeff Simcott wrote.

'Your last letter was most welcome I assure you on behalf of us all here telling us about your preparations for the next phase of your journey. I expect that by the time you receive this, the spring will be here or there rather and you will be past the worst part of the winter in these parts and looking forward to crossing the Jordan into the promised land in a manner of speaking but you will get the drift no doubt. We keep our eyes and ears glued to the wireless these days in the hope that we will soon get news of it all coming to a deserved end and that now that you are all past the worst part of your journey you will soon be arriving at the hallowed gates. Your mum and Mr Marples are well and join me in sending you early

Easter greetings just in case this reaches you when you are in the middle of something as usually happens. Keep looking for the silver lining and the souvenirs.'

By early evening the assault force at Xanten was assembled and ready to go. The river bank was lined with buffaloes, assault boats and DD Shermans and stormtracks and pontoons, and behind them stretched the paraphernalia of the rest of the three brigades: tanks, anti-tank guns, Bren carriers, 3-ton trucks, troops. There was no point in attempting to conceal their activities. The Germans had known for a long time that the allied armies were close behind them and despite all the blowing up of bridges they had done, their precious Rhine had already been crossed at eight points from Remagen to Rheinberg.

'Dear Son,' Jeff Simcott wrote.

'I forgot to add a PS in my last letter because it had to catch the evening post and we had run out of stamps and you know how it is when you least expect it. Poor Mr Marples died suddenly of a bad accident in the factory last week but I have to tell you not to worry about your job when you get back as the business is a family business and in good hands. You get on with what you are doing and don't worry about a thing. You have enough on your plate. Mr Marples' son will be taking over when he gets back from Burma where he has been for some time so there really is nothing to worry about. Your mum and me are fine. Keep up the good work.'

Alabaster had been busy with his pack, taking great care to ensure that his precious cups were carefully protected for the journey. But as the hour of six approached, the deadline for the barrage, he became morose and withdrawn, staring down at the quiet waters, watching the furious assault that was taking place as an army of machines and amphibian craft were manhandled into position.

'Contemplating swimming it then, Simcott?' The sergeant found him pale and pensive on an upturned ammunition box a few yards from the water's edge.

'Could be.'

'Then you take a tip from an old engineer: dinnae cross yer bridges afore they're hatched.'

Alabaster ignored him. 'I don't like the feel of this,' he said, staring ahead. 'We shouldn't be tampering with this.'

'Another one of yer mysteries, is it, Mr Simcott?'

Alasdair stared at the water and drifted off into his Dresden daze.

'Rivers were here long before we arrived', he said, 'running under the ocean. And when the seas pulled back to leave room for the dinosaurs and us lot, the rivers kept their course.'

'Fancy, now.'

'And when we came into the world, we settled along them. So they governed us, winding their ways across the earth like lines on your palm, lines of destiny telling the earth's story.'

'Ah ken what ye mean, tho',' said Sergeant Macintyre of Musselburgh. 'Ever seen the Forth Brig?'

'We were shipwrecked when the world began,' Alabaster went on, 'washed up like flotsam from the great wreckage of the ocean and we had only these spars of the craft left to cling to and remember and focus on, like holy guidelines.'

'I thought there was something awfy familiar about you,' observed Sergeant Macintyre. 'You sound just like my minister.'

'When the oceans pulled back, the rivers were left to nourish us in body and spirit. That's why every people needs its river, because it nourishes them as well as their land. So, when you take someone's river you are taking something else, something more than just a stretch of his water. You are taking a share of his spirit.'

'Aye, right enough,' said the sergeant. 'There was a story in the *Wizard* about that, Red Indians worshipping rivers and so on. The Mississippi and the Nile or something . . .'

Alasdair stared on across the waters as if searching the wigwams on the far side for signals.

'But what's that got to do with Dresden pottery, Simcott?' asked the sergeant.

'Same thing. These people have their own clays and rivers to worship. Our china figures and rivers all carry our life blood. I can't tamper with these things here, their Loreleis and their mythological maidens. I can't tamper with their *Rhine*.'

'Hot stuff, Simcott. You should have stayed in your kiln.'

'I didn't hesitate when my turn came,' Alasdair stared on at the puffs of smoke rising from the far side. 'I didn't stand idly by. But now, who's winning?'

'Don't make no difference to the likes of us, Simcott. Don't make no difference who wins.' Sergeant Macintyre picked up a pebble and tossed it high into the water. Strangely, the splosh sounded above the general din. 'I mean,' he went on, 'you'll still be a piddling potter, won't you.' The first shells of the bombardment whistled past them. 'And me a fucking sergeant.'

Three thousand five hundred guns opened up at six o'clock. Two hours later they were still at it, and the first assault troops were getting ready to embark.

'You coming then, Simcott?'

Alabaster had sat rigid on his box throughout the barrage, hands cupped over his ears, arms tucked into his neck. Sergeant Macintyre shook him back. Alabaster dropped his arms and looked around at the gathering battalions. 'Not that way,' he said, shaking his head.

'Please yourself,' said the sergeant. And looking around added, 'No a bad evening for the time of year.'

Alabaster kept staring at the water, then sighed deeply as if mustering up strength to take some action.

'I don't suppose the post has arrived yet?' he asked obliquely.

Sergeant Macintyre looked at his watch and then up at the first stars. 'Bit early, isn't it?'

Alabaster said, 'Well, it varies a lot in these parts.'

'True.'

Odd salvoes were still whistling past, as if some guns had been late in starting and still had to get through their quota.

'You could try swimming, I suppose,' said Sergeant Macintyre as Alabaster continued to contemplate and, his sighs apart, showed not the slightest sign of moving. 'Six hundred yards. Nine feet deep. Current'll carry, though. But with a bit of luck you might make it before the North Sea.'

By half past eight the bombardment had eased completely and Alabaster was on his feet, flexing, testing his pack. He watched the engineers struggling with their pontoons and the artillery with their guns. A long line of depressed pioneers were filing back and forth to the craft humping boxes of stores and ammunition like chain gangs at twilight in a Russian documentary about workers along the Volga.

Suddenly Alabaster turned and rasped, 'They can have open cities, can't they? Why not open *rivers*?'

The sergeant said, 'Good point. We should bring that up.'

Alabaster bent down and started to empty his pack. 'People are going to need this after the war, you know,' he said, 'just as they've needed it for centuries.' His few items of clothing and shaving gear lay on the wet pebbles. 'Got nothing to do with war.'

He took off his pullover and thick serge shirt and meticulously wrapped up the two cups and replaced them in the bag.

'You gonna try all that spiel on Fritz,' said the sergeant. 'Think you'll convince him to pack it in?'

'Someone has to do something, Sergeant.'

Alabaster hitched his sack on his shoulders and strapped it around his waist. 'I mean, this can't go on for ever, can it?'

'Think he'll listen?' asked the sergeant.

'I got something to show him.'

Sergeant Macintyre of Musselburgh peered at his watch. 'We're going at two, Simcott. That gives you five hours. Just over a hundred yards an hour. Should manage it.'

Alabaster turned to the water and walked to the edge muttering, 'You can't just go around tampering with stuff like this!' he said, and he hitched his pack with its precious cargo.

Following him to the edge, the sergeant said, 'It's only bloody *water*, you know!'

'Not *bloody*, Sergeant! *Holy*!'

Alabaster walked into the water.

'Oh, that reminds me,' said Sergeant Macintyre. 'Hold on a minute.'

Alabaster paused and looked down at his feet but didn't turn. Sergeant Macintyre of Musselburgh squelched and crunched to join him.

'Your mother was never homesick like you said she was,' he whispered. 'There's no such thing as home-sick north of the Border, see?' And tapping Alabaster's shoulder, he added, 'Homesick's for fucking nancies. Your mother was *hame* seek. And *hame* seek's part of your fucking mystery, see? And don't you ever forget that.'

The last they saw of Alabaster he was fighting his way into midstream, and the last they heard was his shout, 'Got nothing to do with war, this.' Splash. 'Go fight your bloody war elsewhere!' Glug.

ENEMY ACTION

North of Berlin, April 1945

Nine

Not far from Berlin at last, Huckleberry Flynn confessed to Sparks, 'I used to dream of this in Coventry. Well, Stoke Aldermoor, actually. I used to think of it as this great sprawling ruin of a place, just like Coventry when we went up to see the rubble, only bigger. And I thought, I knew all along that's why I had to get here!'

Long before the Second Front opened in June 1944, in the days when the Russians were falling deeper and deeper back into their own homeland and the American plan for the invasion of Europe was a Hollywood producer's cigar dream, the Allied world envisaged the end of the war as a military marathon race to Berlin between the Russians and the Yanks. They were the two mighty powers. The Russians would withdraw far enough to entice the Germans into the frozen grip of their infernal winter and watch them die by slow refrigeration; and the Americans would sort out the military and moral chaos they had been bewitched into in the Far East by Japanese perfidy and potency; then they would both turn and strike at the one who had started it all. From that moment the race would be on for Berlin.

But nobody ever told Huck in Coventry. 'Well, Stoke Aldermoor, actually.'

*   *   *

The idea that he would go and see Berlin for himself and send back pictures of what we were doing to them in return for what they had done to Coventry came to Huck when he was rummaging around the shed at the bottom of the garden in Stoke Aldermoor in November 1940. Stacked neatly in a corner were all his brother Henry's photographic materials because that had been his hobby until he went off to join the Navy not long after the Blitz. 'Never seen the sea but it must be a lot healthier than this stinking hole, cooped up like rats and covered in soot you can hardly breathe.'

Henry had an enlarger stand and jars of chemicals and empty bottles and trays ranged along three shelves, and under them boxes of paper in yellow envelopes, wooden frames with heavy fixing clips, clear glass picture frames, and folders crammed full of sheets of crinkly, sectioned paper with dark negatives shining through. Each group was marked menacingly: **DON'T TOUCH** or **HANDS OFF** or **JUST DARE**.

Below stood two large porcelain kitchen sinks rescued from the ruins of two large Victorian houses that had burned down on Bonfire Night the year before as a result of a backfiring Catherine-wheel and hadn't been rebuilt out of respect for those who had died in it.

Huck had helped Henry to drag them home on a makeshift cart and it took hours to cover the half mile because they were solid porcelain. Henry mounted them on bricks from the same ruin and ran a hose to them from the tap on the outside house wall and dug holes into the ground for buckets to take the water when he was rinsing his prints. Huck helped with the construction, or rather watched, fascinated, but never really knew what was going on and then, just when he was getting more interested, along came the war and off went Henry shortly after the Coventry blitz leaving behind all his precious materials carefully stowed away and covered with dire warnings about the dangers awaiting any mischievous fingers.

Berlin fell to the Russians of course. After a nine day battle for the city the Germans finally surrendered the *Reichstag* on the evening of Monday 30th April 1945.

'Not much more they could do,' observed Sparks, setting down his headphones and blowing away cigarette ash dropped by the handful of disinterested British squaddies leaning on his truck at *Stand Easy* somewhere in north Germany.

After a few awkward minutes while more fags were handed around and matches scratched, Huck said, morosely, 'Berlin's fallen then?'

'Looks like it,' said Sparks, settling his dials.

'They planted flags then?'

'Sounds like a real graveyard to me,' said Sparks, winding up leads and coils and buttoning down flaps and pockets as if bedding down his first-born. 'Not much left to plant flags on, I should wonder.'

'No,' commented Huck. He was the only one of the group to express even the slightest interest and even that was blighted.

Huck had planned his war on being in Berlin first.

When he was called up, Henry wasn't allowed to become a photographer in the forces and develop his great talent. He was defeated by fundamental army philosophy: Never allow a man to do what he is good at. Discipline him by testing his fibre and calibre on the exact opposite. It will either break his spirit or make him. Either way you weed out the worst and get an obedient force.

So Henry joined the Navy and became a stoker instead which they told him was 'pretty much the same' as it was all about 'seeing things done properly'; and as Huck knew nothing about the mystery of Henry's craft, he kept his mischievous hands to himself even when he got letters from Henry in Trincomalee and knew he was unlikely to turn up suddenly at the weekend and catch him in the act of rummaging.

Then, after one of his numerous visits to see the sights of the devastated Coventry Cathedral, Huck yielded and rummaged around Henry's shed, and got the first inklings of an idea: if the war was still going when his time came, he would get himself to Berlin and take pictures of the ruins there and send them back – 'for Henry and Coventry. Well, Stoke Aldermoor, actually.'

When he got to Berlin his pictures might make people back home in Coventry feel better about their rubble, because he knew they needed to feel some kind of revenge, if only because they guarded the precious stuff and put a cordon around it as if to preserve it like a monument, and they even boasted about it like the Italians did about their Roman ruins. But Huckleberry Flynn would show them that war does the same thing to everyone.

'Right,' he thought, closing the door to Henry's shed, 'that's *my* war sorted out, then.' And he went off back up the garden path and forgot all about it.

Somewhere in north Germany – or was it east Holland? – Huck found himself hoping that the Russians would win the race to Berlin, not because he was anti-American, but because their homeland had been devastated in a way that neither the Americans nor the British would ever be able to comprehend. And because, somewhere around Caen in France, it was beginning to come clear to him that, whoever won the race, it would not be the British, and whoever was the first man into Berlin it wouldn't be Huckleberry Flynn.

'It was one helluva blow,' he confessed to Sparks searching his dials to find if anyone was out there, 'but I grew up then.'

He heard the latest crackling and waited patiently for Sparks to decipher.

'Sad thing was I only decided to come to war at all because I'd been conned!'

Sparks was deep in his ethereal quest and, enclosed in massive ear-blocking headphones, was hearing nothing of Huck's words anyway. But it didn't trouble Huck. The pair had established a relationship since Normandy, and Huck believed 'you didn't always communicate through the earwaves'.

'I thought the war was between Churchill and Hitler, and that devastation was what had happened to Coventry and Berlin.' He still couldn't come to terms with the messages that the race for Berlin was nearly over and that he hadn't even been entered. He had cultivated a very special interest in and relationship with the German capital during those long years of growing in Stoke Aldermoor. 'Best years of my life,' he confessed to Sparks's headphones. 'Then I get to Normandy and discover the deceit that's been going on behind my back all that time. Heart breaking.'

Huck began travelling up to Coventry with his pals just to see what 'enemy action' had done, or could do. 'Enemy action' was another one of those jargon sayings you heard all the time like 'broke out' and 'fit for heroes', except that you couldn't see them, no more than 'hope and glory' or 'broad uplands'. But it was different when 'enemy action' arrived in Coventry.

'Everything was being destroyed or damaged by "enemy action", you see,' he told Sparks who had not been home since 1939 and probably didn't know much of what was going on in the world outside, 'not just us, everyone, all over the world, and when we heard that "enemy action" had been doing things to our city too, a few of the gang thought we'd better get up there and have a shufti around for ourselves to find out what this thing was all about, get my own view of it all, see? "Perspective" was the word.'

'Funny, we never thought that people had been killed, that there had been dead bodies in that rubble 'cos they were all gone by the time we got there. Which was a bit disappointing really because we had sort of hoped we would see something real for a change. All we ever saw or heard about dead bodies was in comics and papers and magazines, and of course they were all Germans or Russians, never any of ours. The jargon was we were always "taking casualties" and that lots of our chaps were going "missing" or they had "failed to return"; but no one ever told us what had actually happened and what a missing bloke or a casualty or a failed returner looked like. All we ever saw was torn-up countryside and twisted tanks and rubble in places like Coventry.

'That was the First Lie.'

As the dreary days in northern Europe wore on and he plodded his weary way through the Low Countries and north Germany with his regiment becoming more and more jaded by the metre, Huck listened keenly if enviously on Sparks's Heath Robinson handset to reports of the real war on the Eastern Front and in the south. He didn't actually listen himself as Sparks was very jealous of his headset and was obsessively particular about letting anyone else have even the merest crackle of a listen – 'you can get ear problems, you know. You can never be sure where a man's ears have been or when he last washed them after use.'

But Sparks passed on whatever news he could pick up, grateful that someone was at last interested in his profession, the art and craft of dial searching, and grateful too that he was back once more to his real hobby of tuning into the world out there and not just passing on dreary ops messages from one tiring CO to another. He was getting quite a kick out of this new challenge from Huck, monitoring the progress of the Americans and Russians through searching for signals right across the continental spectrum.

'My range goes far beyond the BBC, you know, and the meagre wavelengths of the local military,' he confided in Huck once the relationship was established and the mutual advantage recognised and declared.

Huck and his gang would mosey around the rubble of Coventry Cathedral, dodging the tin hats and getting told off by dark blue wardens to 'watch out there' in case 'you get yourselves done in', tho' they couldn't see how they could get hurt when everything was on the ground anyway: 'not much chance of anything else falling, looked as if it had all fallen already. But you know these official chaps: soon's they put a uniform on they get all god almighty and look you up and down and ask your age – "*real* age" they always says, like a challenge – as if you should have been at the war anyway because you looked old enough, and not hanging about in someone else's rubble.'

Getting pushed off the Coventry rubble was nothing new. They were always being told off for trespassing on other people's property. Couldn't walk anywhere in the country, on the paths outside the village, or anywhere up in town, alleyways and waste grounds, without someone screaming at them to get off his land or his private property and shouting 'like you was a criminal just because you were there. And now when this here "enemy action" reduced your own Cathedral to a pile of rubble it was still someone else's property and they guarded it like it was the Houses of Parliament. We got a thing about property in this country. One of the reasons I went in the end.'

'That was the Second Lie.'

*　　*　　*

Huck had all but given up the idea of beating the Russians to Berlin by Arnhem. By that time it wasn't difficult to figure out that the British were taking the high road to Germany and Berlin and the Yanks the middle and the low. He had seen 'the lie of the land from Normandy'.

The propaganda that had pushed and plagued him through four years of war and finally compelled him to take up arms and come was elementary: the Second World War was a struggle between Britain and Germany. Everyone else was insignificant or incidental, even the Yanks and the Russians. All the others had either caved in anyway or were only popping up at the last minute to take the limelight and the glory from the lone heroics of the British. But he had hardly got off the beaches at Normandy before it was revealed to him that someone had been pulling the wool over his eyes.

Huck noticed the Yanks were everywhere, and that there were an awful lot of them. But equally there was an awful lot of territory to cover between Normandy and Berlin and they alone had the men and equipment to cover it. Huck's side obviously didn't. And it wasn't only Sparks's dilapidated handset that convinced him. 'Symbolic, though.'

No doubt that was why they'd been shoved up north to see if they could do anything about getting into Germany by the side door. News kept coming in that the Americans were racing on direct to Berlin to get there before the Russians. The Eastern Front had caved in and the Germans were being swept back by the weather and the Red Army.

'I worked out Berlin for myself. Got very bored very quickly, I did, rumbled them early on, all that glorious rubble stuff. Someone had to go and show that others were getting a bit of the "enemy action" too.'

'Lost it,' said Sparks, flicking switches and peeling off his headphones.

'They packed up for the night then?'

'Nope, reception's bloody hopeless. What were you saying?'

'I worked out Berlin for myself.'

'Oh.'

'I mean, everyone was saying I'd have to go when my time came, but no one ever gave a good enough reason. It was all that "God and King and Country" jargon, and I couldn't make head nor tail of it.'

'Too much activity,' said Sparks, exasperated. 'Air waves keep jamming. And all them bleeding buildings.'

'You daren't say anything of course.'

'Well, it's not always so bad, I have to admit.'

'Right. And everyone was pretty touchy about it, mostly because they all had "brave boys" who were always in "the thick of it" and you couldn't remind them they were out there bashing their bleeding brains in for a load of sentimental old rubbish.'

'Sometimes you just have to give up,' said Sparks. 'Let everything cool down. Can't always get through, you know.'

'Even so I didn't reckon I'd have to go. But when I did I'd got my goal.'

Sparks settled his aerials like a fisherman packing his gear. 'Proper signaller's nightmare,' he sighed.

'Just didn't know it had all been based on four years of con anyway.'

'Well,' sighed Sparks, flicking the odd switch. 'Three years in the desert don't half spoil you.'

Huck had to wait a long time to go to war, so long that when his call-up papers arrived he had almost given up the idea of going at all. The rubble up in Coventry had long since become old hat, and down in Stoke Aldermoor the war had become a crashing bore and had stopped figuring in his plans. He had even forgotten his pledge. He had been far too busy growing up, and trying to ignore the 'constant barrage' of war jargon and come to terms with the fact that everything was probably a lie anyway. 'You couldn't tell, could you? Who could you believe? No one. *What* could you believe? Nothing. Everything had to be a lie or a deception just to *win* the damned thing. That was OK but it still didn't stop you not being able to believe anything.' So he shut the war out.

When he got over the shock of his papers arriving he couldn't even remember how he had planned to desert, and where he had planned to go. He had made secret plans once and knew the Hebrides figured in them somewhere, but by Christmas 1944 the details if not the idea had gone. It had something to do with the war taking so long. After that first year when he was nearly drowned in propaganda in everything he heard and everything he read, he had shut it out. Course he knew it was there, no one couldn't, but so was bad weather in the Midlands. It was everywhere, but you got that you didn't notice. War had bored the hell out of Huck.

Then he remembered his pledge. Pledge? 'Well, not so much a pledge as a fad, the kind of thing you have when a kid, like one day you want to be a football player when you grow up and the next an engine driver, and then a cricketer in Australia and a Mountie in Canada. You play around with the idea for a few days, then your eye catches the photograph of a pilot or a man with a shade over his eyes and you want to fly a Spitfire or write the *Daily Express*.' But it came back to him when his papers arrived, 'not knowing anything about photography thought I might get to be a war correspondent with a camera instead of a stoker with an oil cloth.'

He helped himself to Henry's Box Brownie and nicked

some rolls of film buried under the floorboards and wandered around the ruins of Coventry Cathedral surprised they were still there, and he took pictures so that when he arrived in Berlin he would take matching pictures and send them back so that they could see that we had done something about avenging that early bombing. Some of his original idea of that peaceful purpose might still come through too.

But of course it depended on getting to Berlin first.

As each day passed and news of the Russian–American race flickered and sparkled on Sparks's set, and vibrated his headphones, Huck was getting the other message loud and clear: that the hope of his own triumphant entry into Berlin at the head of the victorious Allies was running a bit thin.

It was becoming clearer by the crackle that the great twin props of Home Front propaganda had been entirely false: Churchill and Monty were not the only ones fighting Hitler and the British were not going to Berlin first. And now it seemed that Huck was not to become a photographer anymore than Henry: his treatment of old Mr Pickering was threatening to prove unforgivable.

Huck grew more humble and subdued, and if Sparks had difficulty in holding either the fast-riding Yanks or the rampant Russians on his receiver, he was getting messages from Huck louder and clearer by the hour. Huck was taking the inevitability of victory very deeply indeed: staring him straight in the downcast face and screaming at him straight down his unprotected ear holes. It must be much more than disappointment at missing the show.

Sparks had a long experience of war. 'Been tapping out morse long before the cartographers took any interest in Dunkirk.' And the one item of certainty he had observed in the otherwise unpredictable game of war was that whoever had been in one battle, however insignificant and minor, immediately dropped the urge to be present at a second. Sparks had been at a few 'in my time' but he had never yet met anyone who had wanted to have a second go. The guaranteed reflex reaction of any man at the conclusion of any piece of action, however secondary, was the pure and eloquent: 'Stuff that for a lark!' It was not an individual reaction so much as a textbook response, as if 'drilled into every member of the PBI from the moment he joins up'.

But there was something about Huck's doom that went beyond either the heroics or disappointments of battle. Not getting to Berlin ahead of the Russian or American hordes was not about losing face but of losing faith.

Huck studied hard with the aid of materials and books in Henry's garden shed but after four years the materials were past their best. He sought the help and advice of Henry's mentor and sometime employer – 'who taught me all I know' – the ageing Pickering the Photographer who had learned his trade in the studio before the First World War and practised it in the open air at Passchendaele. Since then he had done all the local christenings and weddings and school portraits, and on a tripod with a cover over his head, except that they were rare now that film materials had become scarce like everything else in the days of 'increasing austerity', another ear-catching saying that made Huck puke. But he stuck it out and Mr Pickering was kind and helpful, if sparing and exacting, and taught him in particular how to use his Box Brownie and what to look for.

Mr Pickering's prize possession was a 35mm Leica camera which he had brought back from Germany between the wars because, although he had 'fought the bastards' and 'would willingly do so again', he had to admit they were fine precision engineers who had developed this incredible new camera which fitted into the palm of the hand and on which he had spent all his limited fortune. Although he would probably never ever use it, he having been trained on bigger formats, he could see it as a thing of the future, 'a thing of beauty and a joy forever,' a true feat of craftsmanship. 'You have to hand it to them,' he said, delicately replacing it in its velvet-lined box.

Mr Pickering allowed Huck to stand by his side in the dark-room but he wouldn't give him a precious roll of film until he was 'ready to go solo'. Instead he dispatched Huck to Coventry with orders to wander around the ruins of the cathedral and find twelve different pictures, find them and study them through the window of the Brownie and make sure he had the right frame; and do it again and again and again until he was certain he had selected the best twelve and only twelve that he could see; and then come back to him and describe in words exactly what he had seen and what he would have taken. And Huck obeyed and found it weird taking pictures without a film and going back and pretending that there had been one and finding the right way to describe what he had 'taken' rather than showing Mr Pickering the results. But he got the hang of it after three trips and on the fourth was given a real film and took his twelve carefully worked out 'snaps'.

Mr Pickering developed them in his dark-room and under his very eyes Huck saw his chosen black images emerging on the white paper floating in the tray of developer. He felt exhilarated and much closer to Henry, although when he last heard of him he was safely in the Philippines helping General MacArthur.

Mr Pickering sent him on another trip, or 'assignment' as he now grandly termed it, this time to find the twelve best photographs of well-known Coventry buildings. 'Twelve different buildings and no postcards, mind.

If you've seen it before on a picture or postcard, then don't take it. Stop. Go around it and find another angle, another way of looking at it.'

After three more trips Mr Pickering gave him another roll, and he did the same and found himself watching twelve more pictures emerging through the developer and heard Mr Pickering say he was 'getting the hang'.

He went on a third assignment, this time to 'cover' an actual event. Huck went to a wedding one Saturday and a children's open-air picnic the next and found more ways of seeing except that this time everyone was moving and he didn't have time to compose himself or his shots and Mr Pickering said, 'Ah, that's exactly how it was at Passchendaele. The point and the task is to anticipate, see, and make things happen for yourself. You have to watch and think of what you would like to photograph and work it out beforehand and anticipate and be there and that way you do not leave everything to chance', although happenings were always 'dodgy affairs', like on the Somme.

So when Huck went to war he was as trained as he could ever be given the time and, most important, he knew what he was going to do. He had had, if not an apprenticeship, a splendid training.

'Not quite Henry's standard yet, I'm afraid,' said Mr Pickering. 'Your brother had a gift, you know.' Huck didn't know. 'But you have done very nicely. Yes, one day Coventry may be very proud of you.'

'Stoke Aldermoor, actually,' Huck corrected politely.

'I thought I knew why I was going to war,' said Huck miserably. 'You hear of blokes who never know why they are there, or here. I did, or do.'

'Same's me, mate,' said Sparks. 'And five years in this lot and I still can't figure it out.'

The unit was stuck somewhere north of Berlin, freeing

people and coping with starving refugees and generally mopping up and listening to the reports of the Russians and Yanks closing on the capital. There was a distinct feeling of being out of it now.

'Impetus gone, mate,' said Sparks, taking off his phones and airing his ears. 'That's what it is.'

'But they're not there yet?' asked Huck.

'Near as dammit,' said Sparks.

'But still a lot of fighting to be done,' Huck asserted.

Sparks shrugged. 'Well', he said, 'suit yourself.'

But it affected Huck more than most. He was growing melancholy now.

'Takin' it very personal is old Huck,' observed Sparks, justifying another round of inordinate dial-searching to catch snippets of sputtering news for the forlorn Huck.

'Defence ring around Berlin pierced,' he announced.

Sizzle.

'Zhukov on his way in.'

Sparks held on tightly to his ears and muttered morsels of information in telegramese.

'Throwing a circle of tanks . . .'

Crackle.

'. . . around the holy city.'

'*Holy* city?'

'Siegfried's.'

'Ah.'

The recruiting men asked him what he would like to do and he said photographer, 'preferably in Berlin'. They nodded and said, 'Oh yes, but not many weddings in Berlin these days, so you can be a PBI instead. Much the same really, and just until a vacancy crops up, of course. Then we'll get in touch and transfer you, see?'

Well, that suited Huck and he asked how long it might take and they shrugged and said 'depends, really'. Well,

it was a promise in a way, and he was now in uniform
and ready to go.

Huck kept Sparks going by telling him his story between
crackles and pops.
   'Only thirteen when it broke out ... .'
   'Zhukov's Forty-seventh Army . . .'
   'Broke out! Huh! Like an epidemic of measles!'
   '. . . Konev's Fourth Guards Tanks . . .'
   'Trying to grow up . . . Huh! Trying to learn something
. . . Huh!'
   '. . . only twenty-five miles apart.'
   'What?'
   '. . . only twenty-five miles apart.'
   '. . . on to a hiding to nothing. Huh!'
   'Marshal Rossokovsky . . . north of the city . . .'

He didn't find the training so bad because he managed
to blot out most things just as he had managed to
blot out the previous four years of war and its awful
jargon. This new life charging around screaming and
pushing bayonets into bags of sawdust and polishing
boots and listening to sergeants and corporals shouting
and bawling, and marching around like toy soldiers and
jumping over ditches in full kit seemed all part of the
same nightmare, merely the extension of all those years
of hearing the sayings and listening or trying not to listen
to the voices on the radio and in the cinema all telling
him how wonderful it was to be a hero, and especially
to die as one. He managed to cope, concentrating on
getting to the one place he had come to get to – Berlin;
and to do there what he had decided on that November
morning in 1940 amid the fallen rubble and rising dust
and smoke of Coventry Cathedral – to take pictures and
send them back.
   But they couldn't lend Huck a camera in the meantime

and Huck couldn't afford to buy one and he couldn't take Henry's Brownie because it was too clumsy and fragile to carry around in his kit and besides Henry might turn up any minute after all and he would be bloody annoyed.

They sent him home on leave and promised him he'd be in Germany within a week. On the final night of his embarkation leave, he forced his way into old man Pickering's studio and took his precious Leica from its velvet-lined box, and four rolls of film which he would easily manage to hide in his pack until he reached Berlin.

He consoled himself by pleading that he was doing it for 'a good cause', even a noble one, and that he had not taken the Leica, only 'commandeered' it, and 'in the national interest', and 'in good faith', and for the sake of the 'wider good' – you know the jargon.

'Got fed up listening to that bloke with the posh voice on the wireless telling us how everything we ever had had fallen and we had to "pick ourselves up" and "tighten our belts" and "look for new uplands" and "gleaming horizons" and "keep our chins up" and be "proud of our nation" and "fight on the beaches". Beaches! In Coventry! My arse!'

'. . . held up on the Oder marshes.'

'Where?'

'Oder.' Spurt.

'Who?'

Sizzle. 'Rossokovsky.'

'Oh.' Squirt.

'Sounds like him with the cigar. Always seemed pissed, or chewing something, just like my granddad who got old and couldn't keep his teeth in 'cos they hurt. He sloshed around a lot too, except he just sat in his chair and stared out at the fields all day and read newspapers and never tried to tell us anything about

how to run our lives or our wars because he had nothing
to offer anymore. He'd been in the first one, see, and
didn't want to know about any other, so he just kept on
staring and slushing.'

'Cutting off help from the north.'

'Who, Rostov?'

'Rossokovsky.'

'What help?'

'Hitler's Third Panzers.'

'Glory glory, hero hero, king and country, hope and
glory! You know the jargon. Huh!'

After a nine day battle for the city the Germans finally
gave up on the evening of 30th April 1945. The Russians
had started to shell the *Reichstag* at five in the morning
and went on until after midday.

'How can it stand that length of assault?' Huck asked
Sparks, huddled over his handset somewhere north of
Berlin and east of Hamburg. 'It's only a bloody building!'

Late in the afternoon Sparks held his left hand firmly to
one headphone, screwed up his eyes and raised his right
hand for silence. After a few minutes of agony, twisting
his mouth and eyes, he took off the phones, shook his
head and ruffled his hair, and said solemnly, 'Zhukov's
troops have gone in.'

'Oh,' said Huck, uncertain whether to hit the ceiling
or feel floored.

'After the shelling stopped,' said Sparks softly, 'they
went in. Hand to hand, room to room, corridor to
corridor.' He put his set back on and resumed his search
of the demanding dials.

Late that evening, again huddled over his crackling receiver, Sparks finally took off his headphones
and addressed Huck and the group of bored British
squaddies who had decided to come and lean on his
truck because they were on *Stand Easy*.

'I have to announce,' he said, putting his hands to his bare neck as if adjusting an imaginary bow tie, 'that immediately prior to sunset, double British Summer Time, today Monday, 30th April 1945, two sergeants of the Russian Army raised the Red Flag over the rubble of the *Reichstag*.' He paused, stretched his neck and tie and added, 'Therefore, I declare that hostilities are now ended and that we are consequently in a state of peace with Germany.'

Someone said, 'Cor!' and Sparks added, 'God save the King!'

After a few awkward moments while more fags were handed around and matches scratched, Huck said, morosely, 'Berlin's fallen then?'

'Looks like it,' said Sparks, settling his dials.

Huck was the only one of the group to express any interest and now even that was blighted. It was final confirmation that his war plan had not been achieved.

Huck picked up Mr Pickering's Leica and walked away from Sparks's wagon.

'Where you going, may I ask?'

'Back home to deliver my camera.'

'Can't it wait?'

'Not any more. Held on to it long enough. And Mr Pickering will be missing it. He's not young any more. As long as I was going to Berlin, it was OK. "Pressures of war". You know the jargon.'

'Which direction is Berlin?' he asked a corporal with a map and a compass who was doing nothing but holding them.

'Roughly that-away,' said the corporal pointing to a pile of masonry across the road.

'And Coventry?' asked Huck.

The corporal turned about and pointed to a pile of rubble on the other side. 'Over there, I should say. Roughly.'

'Not much to choose then,' observed Huck.

'Not a lot,' agreed the corporal.

Huck thought for a few moments, sizing up the piles of brick and plaster on both sides. Then he walked off, neither Coventry-way nor Berlin-way but, as Sparks said later, 'in the general direction of off, I should say'.

Half way across a field the sergeant called out, 'That's far enough, Flynn.'

Huck walked on.

'Flynn,' repeated the sergeant. 'I said enough! The joke's over.'

Huck walked on.

After a few moments the sergeant got a bit upset and shouted, 'You heard me, Flynn. Now you get your arse back here at the double!'

Huck kept walking.

After another few moments the sergeant became even more upset and shouted again, 'I warn you, Flynn. Come back or suffer dire consequences.'

Still Huck sauntered on.

The sergeant roared, 'Flynn, I am charging you with desertion! I shall count three and then give the order to open fire.'

Huck stopped and turned. Europe waited.

Huck called back, 'I don't believe you. Any of you!' And swinging Mr Pickering's Leica he turned and walked on.

END CREDITS

Lüneburg Heath, May 1945

Ten

Arriving for the German surrender at Lüneburg Heath on 1st May 1945, Heavy Wates said morosely, 'I should be feeling much happier. But then I never did like Tuesdays.'

When Germany finally got around to surrendering in 1945, she did it all over the place. It was a piecemeal affair, not one grand comprehensive ceremony at the Brandenburg Gate in Berlin with the Germans laying down their arms to the massed forces of Russia, America, Britain and any one else still left standing as they would have done in the movies, but lots of little surrenders: separate rituals in places like Reims and Beaugency in France; Wageningen in the Netherlands; Caserta in Italy; Innsbruck in Austria; Baldham in south Germany and Lüneburg Heath in the north. Monty's one. And of course, Heavy's.

The only reason Heavy Wates agreed to go to war at all was the hope of being somewhere 'significant and strategic' when history was being made. 'No point in going otherwise, is there?' he told his girlfriend Marlene when she asked him if he had a good reason not to go. 'Far less losing your bloody arse!'

Heavy had long since accepted that history always

happened elsewhere, and when it did, never to the likes of him.

'The Pyramids? No, 'fraid they're finished now. The workmen have packed up. Site's all cleared.'

'Bannockburn? Yes, over there, sir, but I think you'll find they've all gone.'

'Waterloo, sir? No, that was fought yesterday, actually. Wellington's gone back now, I'm afraid.'

History was like that. It existed all right. It *happened*. But only once. And you had to be there on time. Take your eyes off it for a second and – woof! – it had gone.

So, when they asked Heavy at the recruiting depot if he had any particular preference for the kind of unit he would like to serve in, he said, 'No, but I'd like to see a bit of history being made, if you don't mind.'

'Do our best,' said the corporal.

On his way in the truck to Lüneburg Heath where the final surrender was going to take place, where Monty was going to have his little last laugh and they were definitely going to 'make history', Heavy was exhilarated. After all these years of pessimism that folks like him always miss out, he would finally be present at history in the making.

He knew exactly what it was going to be like because he had written his own script. 'Can't take chances at times like this,' he said. 'Got to be prepared. Like making movies. They don't just happen. They have to be scripted right down to the last detail. Like battles themselves. Location, sets, lights, stars, extras, got to have them all organised and in place, otherwise sure as hell it'll go wrong, go off like a damp squib. And you can't have history going off like a damp squib, can you?'

Heavy's scenario, which he had worked on for four

years, longer if you counted all his years in the dark
of the local Empire, was built around the twin themes
of trains and goodbyes.

'If you have to make surrender history, for example,
you have to make it in a train, like they did in the First
World War. And it has to be a continental one. Not
just because it's taking place on a continental stage but
because continental trains are built for goodbyes. And
surrender *is* a sort of goodbye, isn't it?'

But when early that Tuesday morning Heavy reached the
little village of Wendisch Evern lying below a hilltop on
Lüneburg Heath, he couldn't detect any sign of a rail
track or a railway station far less a train or a carriage.
His first thought was that they had been sent to the
wrong place but, as the morning advanced, he began to
notice that the place was strewn with patches of ordinary
soldiers and officers and drivers and photographers and
correspondents all making little pocket communities
along the road and at the junction leading to the hill
itself with a solitary caravan and, as far as he could make
out, one largish tent and a few makeshift bivouacs. It all
gave the air of a battalion having halted for a night's rest
except that the scattered personnel seemed to belong to
a variety of different corps and regiments, as if a number
of separate divisions had sent representatives for the
occasion. Heavy was temporarily consoled. The make
up of the groups suggested he was in the right area
if not the exact spot where the great finale was to take
place and the great deed to be done. Obviously it was
not to be done down here in this puny little village or up
there on that forlorn heath, but at least it would happen
hereabouts and Heavy would be present at the making
of history after all.

Of course, it was against all odds. Henry never really
believed his kind could ever get near enough history

to see it being made: 'Real history, I mean. You know, history history, big events, things that get into books.' Henry's experience was that they all happen elsewhere to other people. 'No one you know has ever actually *been* there when they took place, have they? No one you *know*. It's always someone else that gets the break and the glory but never anyone in *your* class or school or street.'

Henry spent his time in school poring over history books with pictures of people in big actions like Harold at Hastings and Bruce at Bannockburn and Napoleon at Waterloo and Hannibal at some other place, but he never thought they were places and events anyone he would have known would have been present at. 'I mean, if they happened today, you know you'd never be there. Other people you don't know would, but never anyone you *do*.'

So when Henry's time to be called up came at seventeen and a half in the autumn of 1944 he went to war only to get a piece of the history, to get near it when they were making it, whatever it turned out to be. And because the war was 'drawing to its close', he thought he had a better chance now than he would have had at any previous time since 1939.

'History's happening all over the place now, isn't it?' he said. 'I mean, before you risked being dumped on some beach or sand dune or mountain or something and left there to slog it out for years without anyone noticing or any chance of a change, but now with things moving at a rate of knots since D-Day, chances are you'll be bumping into history round the next bend.'

He wanted to be somewhere they would write about in books and make movies about, and keep talking and boasting about, 'like them geezers that sit outside pubs telling stories of what happened in other wars, although they always tell you what they *heard* happened, they were never actually there themselves. Second-hand history.' Heavy reasoned that ordinary people get their history second-hand, not just because it happened a long time ago, but because the likes of them wouldn't have been there anyway. Then it's pass it on, or down. 'So we get ours third- or fourth-hand, see, because we always get there when it's finished, like dashing on to the platform when the train's leaving.'

'The Revolution, sir? Closed last week, I'm afraid. Limited run. Not enough bums on seats, really, or bonces in baskets.'

'Trafalgar, sir? Ah, now, you should have been here *last* week. 'Fraid it's all over. Ships back in dry dock.'

'You know the kind of thing.'

When Heavy's platoon was detached from the main group and sent on by truck to take up 'unspecified guard duty' at Lüneburg Heath, the rumour was that things would be happening there soon and that the great bereted chief himself was already installed in his caravan. Heavy had visions of Genghis Khan tents pitched on distant hilltops where commanders dwelt in tapestried splendour surrounded by sabre-brandishing captains and incense-laden mistresses, surveying the battle-locked hordes on the immense plains below. He knew of course that you couldn't expect such middle ages splendour in our modern age but nevertheless a certain *form* of splendour had to be displayed at such momentous times, and he was in no doubt that the high imperial carriages of continental trains would convey something of the same dignity. When someone nodded towards the modest little caravan parked under some bare trees overlooking an army camp site marked by a limp Union Jack on a makeshift pole, he was confused. There was no sign of style or dignity there. His first pang was that he might not be in at the making of history after all. But he quickly convinced himself the nod was in the wrong direction.

On Wednesday morning the news came that British forces had broken through to Lübeck and American forces to Wismar. The Germans now had no hope of returning south and regrouping. Fighting in this sector of northwest Europe had lost its point. Even the proud Admiral Doenitz who had taken over as Head of State when Hitler committed suicide the previous Sunday could have worked that one out.

Until now it had all been very low key. The real buzz started when one of the many war correspondents went about the hill spreading the rumour among the waiting groups that Hamburg was soon to be declared an open city, a sure sign of paving the way for negotiation. Doenitz was not going to defend the great port, but instead would send representatives to meet Monty the following day. But it was still all rumour. Ordinary squaddies never got anything direct. They picked up their scraps from drivers and journalists and the odd hinting sergeant keen for them to believe he had the confidence of captains and things, but nothing open and direct was ever said. Still, all things considered, military events as well as casual encounters, the quiet tone of the surroundings and the hush of expectancy in the air suggested something would happen and it would all be over soon.

Although no one had seen him yet, everyone now knew that the Genghis Khan with the black beret was up there in his drab caravan, hardly a caravanserai as Heavy's scenario called for but fitting the surroundings at least and proof enough that the grand closing ceremony would not be taking place here. Heavy was relaxing, calmly convinced that whatever was to take place in this drab spot it would not be that. It couldn't be. It would not only be a mockery of the Allied triumph, it would be a mockery of history too. And no less of Heavy's own dream.

Heavy needed the war to end in a train. 'Wouldn't have come otherwise.'

He knew when the war started that the First World War had ended in a train. He'd seen the pictures in his history books with the others of Caesar and Napoleon and Harold and Bruce. It had taken its place in his collection of the times history had been made without him. But this time it was authentic. The others were artists' impressions. This was one was genuine – messy, thick, dark, but genuine. Short thick men in long coats and glasses. Wouldn't have thought they knew much about war. Except for Foch of course. And it was his personal carriage. Imagine having a special railway carriage all to yourself!

This time they'd be youngish chaps in berets and peak caps, soldiers settling it for themselves, not bank clerks drawing up statements and balances as if they had had anything to do with mud and trenches and sand dunes and tanks and machine guns. They were pen people. Not this time.

Heavy's epic imagination was a product of the cinema where he had spent most of his childhood: from the long dark double bill evenings of B feature followed by A when any historical event could be recreated, from the sailing of Cleopatra's barge to the departure of Dietrich's express. Heavy had his own idea of how big events looked when they happened, or should look, and how history should be staged.

In the darkened Empire of that childhood and youth, he especially loved the scenes in France or Italy or Germany, or any continental country for that matter, where everyone was always departing and saying goodbye leaning out of windows in tears and covered in mist or steam on railway stations.

And these forlorn people going off into dark, rainy nights at the other end of the platform were always high up in carriages that towered above the station; unlike British carriages where you simply walked straight onboard from the platform – well, near enough – certainly never more than one step, with the result that you had no feeling of 'emotional difference'.

'It's all done on the same level here,' said Heavy to Marlene. 'You can never get lifted up or cast down in these places. Everything takes place on the same plane so that feelings are always flat and tiring, never high and exhilarating.'

And the night. British goodbyes were always said in daylight, so they never had in them the power and passion that dark continental evenings gave – Paris, Berlin, Vienna, Prague, Warsaw, Rome.

'It doesn't mean the same to say goodbye on a British train,' he said. 'It's not visually and emotionally strong enough with the windows at eye level. Continental ones force you to look up in despair and agony or down in pain and agony. And whoever is in the compartment behind the window is always clutching at the frame as if caged, as if being dragged away and up on a kite-string, lifted off into clouds of mist and steam into . . . well, yonders in fact. That's it! Continental goodbyes are about *yonders!*'

Heavy and his tiny group were now assembled on the rim of the hill with a grandstand view of the proceedings: the many restless stragglers and, rarely, the placid Monty. They had obviously been chosen to play an important role in whatever was going to happen, although no one told them.

In the tension of his nagging anxiety, Heavy reassured

himself that even if the surrender did take place here in the next day or two it would obviously have to be *signed* formally elsewhere. Such a tatty little spot had nothing of the right decor or dignity for the final surrender in a war to end all wars.

All morning the atmosphere was quietly building up to something as Heavy studied the quiet movements of cars and the slow gathering of correspondents and photographers and officers and men wandering around quietly and stopping to converse in meaningful huddles.

Then what looked like more official delegations started to arrive, parking down below and trekking up to the bleak heath which Heavy conceded was adequate for Macbeth and a few daggers and shady witches but not at all suited for big historical events. But what mattered was that he was here and, judging by the general state of affairs, north, west and east, it looked as if at long last the Jerries had had their innings.

Heavy had a thing about yonders too. 'Yonders are aspects of goodbyes,' he told his girlfriend, Marlene. Her real name was Janet but Heavy gave his girlfriends names after the stars, so that behind him lay, and occasionally stood, Claudette, Greta, Carole, Simone, Bette, Vivien, Madeleine and Ginger.

'You can't just be what your parents decided. You have to be your own person,' he told each one.

'Or yours?' asked Marlene.

'That's different. Anyway, yonders are extensions. The goodbye is what's happening in the scene. The yonder is the place you are goodbyeing to.'

Yonders meant the fleeting looks and agonised upward gazes and painful downward ones that indicated the darkness at the end of the platform. Again British stations got lowish marks in Heavy's assessment. 'British trains just chug off further along the same track, like an extension of the platform. They don't disappear into distances and darknesses and steams. The yonder element is simply not there.'

British yonders were based on sound – the chuffing of steam and the whistles and the hoots. 'Very good in fact except they don't have the real yonder pictures to go with them.' Not that continental trains didn't have good sound, but Heavy's point was that they didn't need them so much on account of having good yonders to disappear to. 'They have their own inbuilt farewellness.' In any case you couldn't decently, romantically, artistically say goodbye eyeball to eyeball, if you were only going to move along the platform. You had to have the feeling of being separated, in two dimensions, up and down, and of going away and being torn away, a sort of double wrench with a different place to go to. 'Remember Garbo in *Anna Karenina* and Dietrich in *Shanghai Express*? They were truly goodbyes. They had the true touch of the yonders.'

'And *Wagon Train*?'

'No, that wasn't continental.'

Each time an incident happened, a car appearing, a lone officer wandering over to the caravan, a frisson moving a group on the slope, Heavy wondered if it would be now, and after a few hours he began to grow uneasy that the time apparently seemed to be approaching and there was no indication they were to move elsewhere to a place of greater dignity. Even if an ordinary bloke like himself was finally to be allowed to be present at the making of history, it was pretty obvious they wouldn't consider him important enough to inform him, certainly not put him on any guest list.

He began to argue with himself to keep his spirits up. The ending of the war was a kind of goodbye. Even if everyone wanted it to happen and to get it over and done with and get the hell out of the place, it was an ending, a farewell, a goodbye. 'An end to something that has brought people together, in a manner of speaking.'

Another group of Germans moved off down the hill to the Mercedes and the silence hung again and it was raw and it was north and nothing very much was happening, no guns, no trucks, no brass, no flags, no gold braid, no swords and sashes, only the crunch and squelch of boots coming and going and the quiet purring of Mercedes wheels as another group came and went.

'They'll have to go out in style,' Heavy told himself, stomping his feet which were cold on the damp soil. 'They'll have to have their train. Like in the First World War. Chantilly. Foch's personal carriage. They knew about endings.'

Then another group appeared, silently, humbly, coldly. Low voices, low-key saluting, more huddling and rubbing of gloved hands, and pointing to Monty's place.

It was no coincidence they had chosen a train carriage to do it in 1918. They were of the old school, still going into battle in full uniform and on horseback. Still brandishing sabres and polished helmets. Still all pride and plumes. Knew a bit about chivalry too, they did. However mad and out of date, these blokes had style. Been a shambles of a war, it had. Ypres, Somme, Verdun. Millions of chaps just blown away. Flower of manhood, they were. But like the charge at Balaclava, it still had a place for the plume and panache. Style, that's what Foch's carriage was – style.

Now Monty coming out and more movements, shrugs, pointings, shufflings, head shakings, and Monty going in again. Quite a little mime, not necessarily panto type but mime because only the murmurs carried not the actual words, and even the small gestures seemed exaggerated because there was nothing else to take in.

'When Napoleon surrendered to Wellington at Waterloo', Heavy continued his meditation, 'it would have
been better in a train. Come to think about it, with a
name like that, it should have been. Or when Hannibal
handed over his club to Caesar or Edward his axe to
Bruce. Great goodbyes, they were. But just think if they'd
had trains!

'Imagine Hannibal climbing up them steps to shake
hands with Caesar on the Orient Express. Or Wellington
and Napoleon signing in a Pullman. Think of Caesar
leaning out of the window waving the thumbs-up sign
to Hannibal. Or Bruce seeing Edward off at Stirling East
waving his spider-web.'

Again the peace descended upon the group on the
hillside and there was nothing much to do except stand
around and smoke and clump your feet when it was
damned tedious and not a little worrying.

'Human beings are all about goodbyes,' Heavy told
Claudette and Marlene. 'Goodbyes are part of the human
condition,' he told Carole and Ginger.

He knew. He had been saying goodbye for at least five
years. Evacuated three times and returning home, taking
leave of his mother three times and his foster parents
three times, that was six for a start. And saying goodbye
to his dad when he was twelve, that was another one.
And then his two brothers. That made nine in all. And
then the odd uncle and cousin thrown in or wrenched off
into mist and steam on platforms, albeit British eyeball to
eyeball ones. None of them were ever *real* goodbyes with
the high wave and the tears dripping down from above.
But nine of them, not to mention Claudette, Greta, Carole,
Simone, Bette, Vivien, Madeleine and Ginger. He knew.

And as he had spent most of his spare time in cinemas
watching Dietrich and Garbo and Gable and Davis saying
goodbyes on international trains, and in dramatically

dismal black and white, never cheerful colour, he was well steeped in the culture of goodbyes.

These blokes who organise wars know the drama and the publicity involved, Heavy reassured himself in the damp and the hush. They know all about the big occasion and how to get the best effect out of a scene. When the end comes and the credits roll, they'll have chosen the right shot, the right spot, no doubt about that, *and* it'll be a train. They'll know about endings. The rest of the war may have been a complete shambles, but they *couldn't* mess up the ending.

As the day progressed, Heavy began to wander about, picking up scraps of information as befitted his lowly position: neither an officer nor an NCO, nor a correspondent nor a photographer, nor a film cameraman nor a bloke with a mike. But there was no talk of the venue, and no suggestion that any of these privileged people considered it of any interest far less significance. That worried him, because he couldn't understand that all these senior and privileged and educated people weren't concerned about the staging and the style of the great event. And yet more and more kept coming: groups of officers, photographers, correspondents, cameramen, chaps dragging cables into the big tent and someone saying he thought they were the BBC.

But no sign of anything else, certainly no railway carriage, and he couldn't get any information about where the nearest railway siding was. He was discovering that he wasn't the kind of bloke others troubled to give information to, so it was all speculation on his part, and he became quite isolated and introspective, drawing more and more on his imagination because no one wanted to talk and discuss with him and help him in his confusion and anxiety.

*   *   *

Heavy had written his own farewell, his own surrender scenario, like a movie script. He had imagined the whole scene at Bamford Crossing when he set off with his brown cardboard case with the lock that kept springing open and had to be tied down like some mad dog.

Of all his many goodbyes this was the one when nobody turned up. The train was only eye-level but nobody was there anyway. His dad had gone to war long before him and hadn't written home for ages and his mum wasn't able to face the tearful parting so she coped with it instead in the back room, and most of his girlfriends had deserted him or were working in munitions factories or on the land. He made his own trek to the Crossing that morning and helped himself to a lonely final goodbye in continental spirit if not carriage, but in fact he was secretly pleased that his mum didn't come to the low-platformed station and ruin it, or rub it in as, carriages apart, there was no tunnel or cutting at the end of the platform to provide a decent yonder for him to go off into anyway.

It had been the same with all these intermediate goodbyes, the evacuation and holiday ones. They had never had the stuff of real farewells in them – *au revoirs*, maybe, but *adieus*, never – so that he had never really felt sad at either the comings or the goings. He put it down to some lack in himself, but he knew now it had been solely because of the setting. He just couldn't get worked up on a British station with a carriage door directly opposite him and leaning out of a window directly into the faces of his mum or his foster-mum or his sister or girlfriends or whoever bothered to turn up. There was simply nothing special about parting. No sense of occasion. Well, at least he had learned this much from war: his feelings were not at fault, only the props that surrounded them.

He was determined to make up for it on the continent where he was bound to get a glimpse, if not a personal experience, of a decent continental goodbye – in the flesh, so to speak – but he never imagined his luck would turn out so brilliantly, that he was actually to be present at the final unconditional surrender, Monty's own good-bye, and so obviously in a train and a continental one at that.

Now he couldn't decide in his scenario if it should take place in First Class or Third, the dilemma being that Monty merited First but the Nazis were definitely Third. In the end he plumped for First because Monty had to take precedence. The Nazis could be invited to come into First from Third but there was no way Monty could be expected to visit Third. They had to come to Monty, not vice versa. They were the supplicants.

And of course it would have to be in the restaurant car where there was room and a table and places for papers and glasses, otherwise they'd have to sit in separate groups and not be able to chat to each other face-to-face; and he didn't see how Monty could be seated and have to shout over his shoulder to the German behind to ask him if he'd mind surrendering now before the next stop.

Up on the heath they were setting the scene at least, getting it blocked and rehearsed and word perfect, everybody off the book, and practising in front of mikes in the tent, the nearest to a drill hall. Actors never rehearsed on the big stage, only in seedy little scout huts and bare training halls before taking the play into the big theatre, so that was obviously what was happening here. The performance, and the pomp and circumstance the performance demanded, came later, with the train.

Around elevenses on Thursday morning a big Mercedes drives up to the top of the heath and four thick German officers get out and an escort takes them over to the caravan.

After a good five minutes while they all look embarrassed and stomp their feet to keep warm 'cos it's still a bit parky, the door opens and Monty appears and makes a sign to his aides around him as if saying: who are these blokes, then? Then the Germans salute and reply and Monty comes down and they stand around and start chatting and Monty moves his hands and arms a bit but the others stay stumm. Or if they do say anything they don't seem to move their bodies but in them damned great greatcoats you never know what's happening underneath. Funny thing is he never invites them in, not even for a cup of char. They just keep on standing and chatting, must be for a good hour or more.

Then, would you believe it, they break for lunch and Monty goes back indoors and the others get taken over to one of the makeshift tents and they have a bit of nosh.

In Heavy's script, after the signing takes place, he positioned Monty and Mob on the platform and left the Germans in the carriage, so that they would slowly pull away leaving Monty and the gang staring after them and saluting stiffly. It would have to be stiffly: no one ever saluted limply. The salute was OK, part of the drama. And the dignity. Soldiers were soldiers all over. Fight each other tooth and nail for four years and yet be quite prepared to shake hands and salute each other when it was all over. Sounded a bit hypocritical, but that's how it was. Something to do with these polished helmets and plumes they all used to wear. Didn't seem to fit khaki or field grey, but that's tradition for you and who was Heavy to complain. In a movie it looked much better, much more dramatic, and that's all that matters. And all that *would* matter in the history books.

After lunch the Germans appear again and walk back

to the caravan and Monty emerges and the whole affair starts once more. Then after another long time two walk down the hill again, get back into their car and drive off while the other two go back to the lunch tent and Monty disappears.

And that's it for the day and it's all quiet and all you can hear is the odd bird and the low murmuring as if they're presiding over a dying. Still no sign of trains or carriages.

Or should it be Monty in the carriage and the Germans on the platform? It's Monty who's going back, the Germans staying. Monty and Co. could go off into the mists and steam. And it might look better if he were looking down and the Germans straining up – more symbolic, more effective. The defeated left below to mop up. The glorious who had come down from on high to sort out the petty squabbles lifting away again into steam and clouds at the end of the platform.

Much better. Endings are all symbolic anyway.

Nothing happens the next morning, Friday, either. No sign of any Germans or cars or even Monty coming out for a breath of fresh air. Just the same groups and journalists.

In the middle of the afternoon the Mercs turn up again, but still no Monty. Some staff officers talk to them and they all get in again and drive off back to the village.

Then at five in the evening they call a press conference, then an hour later they all disperse, and the buzz is it's all over and peace is coming up in a matter of hours, once they get their pencils sharpened.

The German officers line up for their photographs and one really senior geezer is taken into Monty's caravan parked under the trees, the first time a kraut gets over his threshold. Must be something special now. Around half past six the general chappie comes out followed by Monty and suddenly people are waving and pointing to the big tent and the cameramen and journalists crowd around it and the BBC guys brush past them, checking cables, and after three or four days of dullness and coldness and nothing much happening but chats and rumours the whole blasted heath is on fire.

'What's on, then?' asks Heavy and breaks ranks and tackles a journalist who's rushing down the hill, and he shouts over his shoulder, 'It's all over, they're signing now!' And Heavy shouts 'Where?' and the hack shouts, 'In the big tent, there!' and Heavy is stunned, rooted to the ground and history is closing in on him: years of waiting and wondering and writing his scenario, dreaming and imagining and preparing, forming pictures and putting in touches and getting nearer to destiny.

That was really what the war was all about for Heavy: the right setting, the right set, the right design, the right characters, the right emotion, the right drama. Without it all these men would have died in vain.

And he wouldn't be done out of his ending. He hadn't spent ten years in the creative darkness of a cinema to tolerate anything less. He would have his train and his farewell in the only dignified way it could be celebrated. He had invested a lot in this farewell. He knew exactly how it should look.

Now he stands stunned, stunned, stun . . . stun . . . stunned . . . staggered, stult . . . They can't do this to him and history and all those men who went and died and got their arses blown off! And he breaks and shouts out and rushes towards the tent to protest at the terrible injustice done to history and the terrible cutting of his script, screaming treason, and the other guards suspect a plot and the shots ring out and Heavy pitches forward into mists and steam and blackness and horns and hootings and shouts and chuffs and screams and wailing and crying and everything going black . . .

But he sees Monty turn from his place high up in the carriage to look down at the group holding the broken figure left abandoned on the platform as the mist creeps up over the heath, like smoke over the stage or steam over the carriage edging off to yonder, and the screen goes black and the credits roll.

ON YER BIKE, SCHWEIK!

One man's humorous tales of World War II

Eric Davidson

'On August 6th 1945, the day they dropped the atom bomb on Hiroshima, my father turned to the wall on his sick-bed, snarling "On yer bike, Schweik!" – and died.'

For him, Hiroshima had obliterated the margins – the areas created by human error into which the good soldier Schweiks have always escaped and survived.

In 1939 the men who went to war were, for the last time, the Sons of Schweik: the Common Men, the Small Men, the Botchers and the Bunglers. *On Yer Bike, Schweik!* is a collection of stories about some of these fantastic characters for whom war, 'like life, was all make-do and mend, try all and error'.

They are based on the letters a father sends home to his family while serving from Dunkirk to Monte Cassino. They don't talk of war, but of the hapless characters desperately struggling to cope with it: like Gordon Blue, who runs a bacon sandwich cafe in the Mile End Road and dreams of greater cuisinery grandeur; Great Shakes, the poet of the Desert Army who writes verses for everyone, then starts composing for Jerry too; and Con Brio, 'flautist to the eighth' who refuses to fight Eyeties on Berlioz's birthday.

After five years and five wounds, the father returns home to retell his tales, enhancing and embellishing them until they hover around the border between fact and fiction, but always remaining true to their origins: one man's experience of war.

FICTION
0 7515 0867 5

Warner Books now offers an exciting range of quality titles by both established and new authors. All of the books in this series are available from:

Little, Brown and Company (UK),
P.O. Box 11,
Falmouth,
Cornwall TR10 9EN.

Alternatively you may fax your order to the above address. Fax No. 01326 317444.

Payments can be made as follows: cheque, postal order (payable to Little, Brown and Company) or by credit cards, Visa/Access. Do not send cash or currency. UK customers and B.F.P.O.: please send a cheque or postal order (no currency) and allow £1.00 for postage and packing for the first book, plus 50p for the second book, plus 30p for each additional book up to a maximum charge of £3.00 (7 books plus).

Overseas customers including Ireland please allow £2.00 for postage and packing for the first book, plus £1.00 for the second book, plus 50p for each additional book.

NAME (Block Letters) ....

....

ADDRESS ....

....

....

☐ I enclose my remittance for ....

☐ I wish to pay by Access/Visa Card

Number ☐☐☐☐☐☐☐☐☐☐☐☐☐☐☐☐☐☐

Card Expiry Date ☐☐☐☐